Believe in the Magic of Christmas

KATHRYN KALEIGH

THE DEVEREAUXS

(Reading Order)

Red Lipstick Kisses and Small Town Wishes

Stolen Dances and Big City Chances

Chance Connections and Upside Down Plans

A Christmas Kiss on the Twenty-Fifth

Believe in the Magic of Christmas

ALSO BY KATHRYN KALEIGH

Contemporary Romance

Belonging in Alpine Falls

Stranded in Alpine Falls

Believe in the Magic of Christmas

The Princess and the Playboy

A Christmas Kiss on the Twenty-Fifth

Red Lipstick Kisses and Small Town Wishes

Stolen Chances and Big City Chances

Chance Connections and Upside Down Plans

Accidentally Forever

Finding Forever

Forever Vows

Our Forever Love

My Forever Guy

Out of the Blue

Kissing for Keeps

All Our Tomorrows

Pretend Boyfriend

The Forever Equation

A Chance Encounter

Chasing Fireflies

When Cupid's Arrow Strikes

It was Always You

On the Way Home to Christmas

A Merry Little Christmas

On the Way to Forever

Perfectly Mismatched

The Moon and the Stars at Christmas

Still Mine

Borrowed Until Monday

The Lady in the Red Dress

On the Edge of Chance

Sealed with a Kiss

Kiss me at Midnight

The Heart Knows

Billionaire's Unexpected Landing

Billionaire's Accidental Girlfriend

Billionaire Fallen Angel

Billionaire's Secret Crush

Billionaire's Barefoot Bride

The Heart of Christmas

The Magic of Christmas

In a One Horse Open Sleigh

A Secret Royal Christmas

An Old-Fashioned Christmas

Second Chance Kisses

Second Chance Secrets

First Time Charm

Three Broken Rules

Second Chance Destiny

Unexpected Vows

Begin Again

Love Again

Falling Again

Just Stay

Just Chance

Just Believe

Just Us

Just Once

Just Happened

Just Maybe

Just Pretend

Just Because

Believe in the Magic of
Christmas

Chapter One

Emma Flynn

Some would describe the Houston Galleria at Christmas as a magical place, pulsing with the excitement that came with that final week leading up to Christmas.

The hub of it all was the ice-skating rink.

At the moment, the ice-skating rink itself was closed for a live concert with an up and coming musicians who was currently entertaining the crowds with loud, lively Christmas music blasting from the oversized speakers. The music spilled down the wide halls and into the stores.

The fifty-five-foot tall artificial Christmas tree was adorned with 450,000 twinkling lights and 5,000 ornaments. Every year the artificial tree was hand fluffed by a team of volunteers, the whole process starting in October.

In addition to the tree, giant sparkly ornaments hung from the ceiling turning the whole three-story shopping arena into a holiday wonderland.

The first floor, in addition to the ice-skating rink, housed a hair salon, a Mexican restaurant, a hamburger place, and several fast food restaurants. Other eateries came and went.

During the holidays, there were pop up coffee shops and doughnut shops along with booths selling t-shirts, jewelry, and customized gifts like mugs and teddy bears.

Tourists flocked from all over the world just to come here to shop at the Galleria.

They could get everything from the most expensive jewelry in the country to the latest fashion. Legos. Barbies. Handbags.

There was no excuse for a person to not walk out with the perfect gift.

But it happened all the time.

People came in, looked around, got overwhelmed, and walked out with a gift card. Maybe to a specific store. Maybe a gift card they could spend at any place in the Galleria.

I understood those and they had their place.

According to my sister, a gift card was THE best gift. Hands down.

Like me, my sister loved to shop and being gifted a gift card was better than any actual gift. It was a chance to go shopping. The gift that led to shopping, she called it.

My sister and I both agreed and disagreed in that respect.

Personally I believed that knowing a person and going to the trouble to pick out the perfect gift for them—something they would cherish—something they would know was chosen specifically with them in mind—was better than any gift card.

So I braved the crowds in search of those perfect gifts, one for my sister, of course. I'd slip in a gift card to one of her favorite stores along with whatever gift I found for her. She was truly the easiest person to buy for.

I also had to get gifts for my mother, my father, my grandmother, and my aunt.

Some years I came shopping with an idea in mind about what I was going to get. Last year I had come shopping with an itemized list, everything already figured out.

This year I was shopping into the dark. I had absolutely no idea what I was going to get anyone.

Part of it, I thought as I slipped past a young family with three bright-eyed preteen girls. Everything was bright and shiny and new to them.

They still believed in the magic of Christmas.

I was twenty-seven. It was a little hard to still believe in magic at twenty-seven.

Last Christmas had been different. Last Christmas I'd had a completely different outlook on life. I'd been engaged to a perfectly fine accountant that I thought myself in love with. This year I was supposed to be a married woman. But right in the middle of summer during the brutally hot month of July, Edward, his name was Edward, had broken up with me.

He hadn't even had the decency to offer an explanation.

The breakup still stung, but mostly I considered myself to be over him and mostly when I really thought about it, I was relieved that he was no longer in my life.

He had been one of those guys who preferred to spend time with his friends over spending time with me, especially if it involved my family.

He knew I was close with my family going in. The longer we were together, the more resentful he became about me spending time with my family, even though he was always invited.

Yes. It was definitely best that he was no longer in my life.

I had dodged that bullet.

I ducked into a high end clothing store on the second floor. Wandered the aisles, running a hand over silky dresses and cashmere scarves.

My mother was retired. She had no need for silky dresses and she had a cashmere scarf already, that I had given her that she never wore.

To her credit she kept it, folded and stashed neatly in the top drawer of her bureau along with other things my sister and I had given her over the years.

Maybe that was one point for my sister. Maybe my mother would have preferred a gift card that she could have used to get something else. Something practical like a new pair of walking shoes.

My sister preferred casual and athletic. Nothing in here for her either.

I left the clothing store. There were no other shoppers in the store and, to me, that was a red flag. I preferred, especially at Christmastime, to shop in the crowded stores.

It was probably a silly, even invalid sentiment, but it was my own measure of how good a store was. I had come to the conclusion that people only flocked to the best stores.

I stopped at one of the little coffee shops and bought a latte. Maybe a little caffeine would get my creative juices flowing.

Standing at the railing overlooking the skating rink, I checked in with my sister.

Are you finding anything?

After a couple of minutes Zoe wrote back.

ZOE

Found a couple of gifts. Want to have lunch?

Sure. Meet me at the Mexican place?

I slipped my phone back into my pocket and laughed to myself.

At least Zoe was trying to shop for gifts. She was probably buying gift cards, but that was okay. She put time and energy into buying gift cards from places people would like, so that couldn't be minimized.

The thing that I found most amusing was Zoe's love of eating. She barely weighed a hundred pounds, but she ate any chance she got. Not that she ate much at the time. She just ate often.

I took my coffee and continued to wander down the hallway. I stepped into a high end souvenir store and considered getting my father a t-shirt for him to wear when he and Mother started traveling next year.

The t-shirt had a saying on it.

Home is Where the Heart is... and My Heart's in Texas

I decided to think about it. I could always come back to it

later. Part of the fun of shopping was finding things and then deciding what to come back to.

Right now I was in what I called the exploration stage.

There were still six shopping days until Christmas. So I had plenty of time to make last minute decisions.

I stepped onto the crowded elevator with back-to-back people —a woman with a baby carriage, a couple with a child, and several other people—and rode down to the first floor.

The musician had finished her concert and her crew was packing things up. The skating rink staff was busy getting the rink ready to let skaters back out on the ice.

With the musician leaving, the crowd was thinning out a bit, making it easier to walk about.

I gave my name to the hostess at the Mexican restaurant, took a pager, and went back to sit on a bench in front of the skating rink.

They were letting skaters back on the ice now.

For now, however, only the experienced skaters were allowed out on the ice. Performing for the lingering crowd.

They were using them as part of the entertainment.

They were letting Olympic quality skaters entertain people who had come to see the musician.

It wasn't a bad thing. Professional level skaters like that enjoyed getting out on the ice in front of an audience.

They spend most of their lives training for something just like this. This was their chance to get out there on the ice, pleasing the crowds. Taking a bow when they were finished.

It was good practice in case any of them every did make it to the actual Olympics. It could happen. It had happened. We'd had a Houston girl make it. Two of them, in fact.

I watched the skaters with envy. My parents hadn't deemed ice skating worthy of the time and expense it would have taken to send my sister and me to lessons.

Learning to ice skate was not an easy endeavor. It wasn't something just any family could handle.

It was a fulltime job that began in childhood and took a commitment from the entire family.

No. I was probably better off doing what I was doing.

It would have been awesome though to have been able to step out onto the ice and wow anyone who happened to be watching.

I straightened in my wool coat. I was okay doing what I did.

My life had plenty of meaning and not a little bit of recognition.

I was, after all, at the top of my field.

"Hey you," my sister said, coming up behind me. "Please tell me we're in line."

I held up the pager. "Shouldn't be long."

"Have you bought anything?" she asked, sitting down beside me, dropping her two shiny red shopping bags at her feet.

"Not yet," I said.

Straightening her coat, Zoe looked at me quizzically before turning her attention to the skaters on the ice.

"Something is wrong with this picture," Zoe said. "I've bought three gifts. Actual gifts. Not gift cards. And the super shopper herself has bought nothing."

"I still have time," I said. "Besides, if all else fails, I know that at least one person would be okay if she got a gift card."

"What's the world coming to?" Zoe asked with a sigh.

"I honestly don't know," I said. "But don't worry. I'll find something. I'll find something for everyone. I'm not giving up yet."

Unfortunately, I felt far less optimistic than I let on.

I'd give it a couple of days, but I might just end up getting everyone gift cards after all.

I didn't want to admit it, but maybe my Christmas spirit was lagging a bit this year.

Chapter Two

"I'm going to sign you up for a dating app," Zoe announced over tacos.

I picked up my napkin and looked at the stubborn set to my sister's jaw.

"No," I said. "You are not."

"It's been, what? Six months? Since you went on a date."

"I don't have time to date."

The server refilled our glasses of hand-squeezed strawberry lemonade. The lemonade was one of the main reasons I liked coming here.

Zoe sipped her lemonade through a straw.

"Are you sure you don't want a margarita?"

"A margarita sounds good, but you know I'm driving."

"As always," Zoe said as a token complaint. "What don't you just try one of the dating apps?"

"Why don't I not?"

Zoe checked her phone.

"How many of those apps are you on?" I asked.

"A lady never reveals her number," Zoe said primly.

Refraining from further comment, I scooped up a bite of freshly made guacamole.

"Look," Zoe said, holding up her phone. "There are so many guys out there looking for dates."

She showed me a picture of a guy who was unarguably nice to look at.

But in support of the stand I was making, I wrinkled my nose.

She swiped to the next picture.

"How about... a guy with a beard?"

"I don't—"

"Oh look. This guy has a dog."

"I don't know... I'm more of a cat person."

"Picky much?"

I shrugged. "You're the one looking."

Holding up her phone, she scrolled through some more photos.

"You're wasting your time," I said. "I'm on a dating moratorium."

Zoe rolled her eyes. "That's not a thing."

"It's a thing."

"Suit yourself." She laid her phone on the table, the dating app still open to a guy wearing a black turtleneck. No thank you.

"I'll be right back," Zoe said. "Restroom."

"Take your time."

I broke a chip in half and glanced back at Zoe's phone. The guy with the turtleneck smiled up at me, upside down. No... and no.

After I used my napkin to wipe my mouth, my gaze was drawn back to Zoe's phone.

At first I thought the lock screen had come up, but then I realized the photo had changed.

Was it supposed to do that? I wasn't familiar enough with dating apps to be able to answer that question.

Using one finger, I turned her phone around so I could see the picture that was now on her screen.

It was still the dating app, but a different guy.

When the screen started to fade just before it locked, I tapped it to keep it awake.

While I was at it, I pulled it closer.

No. Way.

Absolutely. No. Way.

Zoe slid back into her chair.

"Caught you," she said.

"No."

The look on my face must have alarmed her.

"What is it?"

"Does it change by itself?"

"What do you mean?"

"If you just let it sit there, does it go to the next person?"

"Not unless you swipe it," she said, leaning over to look at her phone.

I looked at my sister, my thoughts going in about fifty different directions.

"I didn't touch it."

"It's okay. I don't mind."

I grabbed her phone and held it up for her to see the image.

She frowned at the screen.

"Is that...?"

"Yes," I said, turning the phone back so the screen faced me.

I studied the blue eyed man with the little smile on his full lips. Smooth skin and a strong chin. Short dark hair.

Wearing a... baseball uniform?

My whole system felt like it just shorted out.

Just shorted out and went on the blink.

Everything about him was familiar.

I knew what it felt like to be on the other end of that blue-eyed gaze.

I knew what it felt like to kiss him.

I knew what it felt like to be in love with this man quite simply because I had never stopped.

Chapter Three

"No," I said.

"You have to let me sign you up so you can talk to him," Zoe insisted.

"Not going to happen."

The server cleared off our table and left the check as my sister and I read Theodore Devereaux's dating profile.

"It doesn't really sound so much like him," I said.

"It sounds like him to me," Zoe said.

I bit my lip and read the profile again. It described him, but it didn't sound like anything he would write.

I knew Theodore. I knew just how private he was.

He would never tell anyone that he enjoyed reading science fiction fantasy novels. I'd discovered it by accident. It wasn't like anyone cared, but at the time he had a couple of friends who probably would have ribbed him about it.

And yet there it was right there on the screen.

I like reading science fiction fantasy novels.

But Zoe was probably right. He'd probably gotten over it. He was a grown man now.

It had been ten years since I had seen him.

And yet... if he was on social media, I hadn't found him. Yes, I might have looked. Who wouldn't? Everyone looked for their old boyfriends or girlfriends on social media at some point.

But if he wasn't on social media, then it was quite possible that he was still private. No matter what anyone said, people did not change that much.

Ten years.

At least it would be ten years in five months.

Close enough.

I remembered our last Christmas together.

I'd known something was bothering him then, but I hadn't realized the significance of it. It was only in retrospect that I figured it out.

"Can I borrow my phone?" Zoe asked, holding out her hand. "I need my credit card."

"Of course."

I handed her the phone and watched as she slipped her credit card out of the back cover and swiped it.

We took turns buying each other meals when we went out. I lost track, so had to just assume that it was her turn.

"Do you want the app on your phone?" she asked. "Just in case."

"No," I said shaking off the haze I seemed to have fallen into.

"Here," Zoe said. "I just sent you a screen shot so you can have his picture."

"I don't need—" My phone chimed with a text from Zoe.

"And I just got a warning for violating the app's terms of service," she said with a little shrug.

"For taking a screenshot?"

"Yep. They're very strict. But this was an exception."

"I don't need a picture of Theodore."

"At least you know what he's doing now," she said.

"I knew what he was doing." But it was just a hunch. I hadn't actually kept up with him.

I was surprised he didn't show up on Google.

If he was a baseball player, how could I not have found him?

"Ready to get back to shopping?" Zoe asked.

"Sure." But I was pretty sure shopping was the last thing I wanted to think about right now.

Everyone in my family just might be getting a gift card from me this year, after all.

Chapter Four

Zoe and I got back to Maple Creek just as the sun was setting over the horizon.

Zoe had an early day tomorrow where she worked in a bakery downtown.

I didn't have an early day, but I had some things I wanted to think about.

After dropping Zoe off at her apartment, I drove to my grandmother's little cottage on the other side of the little town.

The little town of Maple Creek was decked out for Christmas. Colorful lights were strung everywhere. Across every street. Around every door and window. Garland and red bows landed on everything that didn't move and some things that did.

The wooden boxes of ivies lining the sidewalks glowed with twinkling lights.

As I drove through town, I heard Christmas music spilling from the speakers.

The stores were closing for the evening. So different from Houston where the stores stayed open into the night, especially during the holidays.

I had mixed feelings about being back here in Maple Creek, but it had been my choice.

My grandmother was getting up in age and she needed someone to help her take care of things around the house.

Since I worked from home, it was easy enough for me to relocate.

Granted, my sister could have moved in with her, but Zoe didn't have the temperament. And besides that, she was rarely home.

"Grandma, I'm home," I called as I went in through the back door.

"Good," Grandma said. "I could use some help with hanging up the clothes."

"You did the laundry?" I asked. "That's supposed to be my job."

"If you take all the jobs, what am I supposed to do?"

"Just do your thing. Exercise. Watch television. Talk on the phone."

"I did all those things today." Grandma waved a hand dismissively. "I even made some cookies."

"You aren't supposed to use the kitchen." I automatically walked over and checked to make sure all the burners were off.

The last time Grandma had cooked something, she'd forgotten to turn off the oven.

"Don't worry," she said. "I remembered to turn the oven off."

"I know you did." But it didn't keep me from worrying.

"You got a box in today. You ordered something?"

"Just some supplies," I said.

I walked through the house, making sure everything was as it should be.

Whiskers, the cat, had a bowl full of food. His water bowl fountain was full, water tumbling out of the fountain.

Grandma, it seemed, had taken care of everything she was supposed to do while I was in Houston with my sister.

I filled a glass with water and sat down at the kitchen table with her.

"What kind of cookies?" I asked, picking one up.

"Chocolate chip," Grandma said proudly.

"Your old recipe," I said, taking a bite. "As good as I remember."

Grandma beamed.

"What did you do all day?" I asked. "Besides make cookies."

"I took a walk with Doreen. You know all she does is talk. About nothing. I swear I've never known anyone who talks as much as Doreen and never says anything of any importance."

I hid a smile. Sometimes Grandma and her friend Doreen were mistaken for twins.

"We stopped at the Piggly Wiggly for a few groceries. They have their Christmas stuff on sale."

"Sounds like you had a big day."

"Oh," she said, obviously remembering something. "You had a phone call."

I instinctively glanced at the cell phone in my hand. No calls.

"On your home phone?" I asked.

"Yes. He said he'd call back."

My stomach did a little flip. Grandma'd had the same phone number since I was a little girl.

"Who was it?"

"He didn't say. But he sounded like a nice young man."

I didn't give anyone Grandma's home phone number. I used my cell phone only.

Who would try to reach me at Grandma's house?

"It was probably a wrong number," I said, picking up a second cookie. Grandma wasn't supposed to be using the kitchen, but she hadn't lost her knack for baking.

Zoe had most definitely gotten her passion and skills for baking honestly.

Maybe it had been a wrong number. It had to be.

But I couldn't help thinking that the only person who could possibly know where to find me here was... Theodore.

Chapter Five

Emma

I got up early the next morning both out of habit and out of necessity.

In the mornings, for one thing, my mind was clear and I could focus on work. The other thing was my grandmother required a lot of attention once she got up.

I sat at my desk in front of the window in the space my grandmother had cleared out for me. When I had moved in, she had given me a bedroom and she had cleared out what had been my grandfather's study.

My desk, the same desk my grandfather had used for his business deals and bookkeeping faced the window overlooking the front yard.

The occasional car passed by as well as kids riding bicycles. Older people walking.

Grandma's house faced a maple tree lined street just off of Main Street. I could, in fact, walk out the front door, turn left, follow the sidewalk past two other houses, and be right on Main Street. A turn to the right took me down into a winding neighborhood with the high school nestled along one of the many optional turns.

A helicopter flew low, heading somewhere. Probably the hospital. We had an active little airport, what with the Devereauxs flying in and out all the time, but helicopters were rare. Usually a helicopter meant some kind of medical emergency.

Could be a news crew flying up from Houston.

The university was closed for the holidays and I had all my grades turned in.

It was always such a relief to get that last grade turned in. For Fall semester, it meant that the holidays were officially here.

It also meant that I could take a break from lecture preps, test preps, discussion board grading, paper grading. The list went on and on.

Except that I didn't really get a break.

Next semester starting in January, I was going to be teaching statistics. A brand new prep for me.

I had yet to meet anyone in my field who actually wanted to teach stats. Statisticians were out there, of course. But as rule, clinical psychologists like me, even clinical psychology professors weren't fond of statistics. That was why it was on a rotation so none of us got stuck with it on a regular basis.

It was my turn on the rotation, so I had to start from scratch.

I could have used someone else's notes. Everyone who taught it before me offered their notes and presentations, and tests, but that wouldn't help me. Not in statistics.

I had to start from the beginning on a complicated topic like statistics or I wouldn't be able to teach it. After I broke it down for myself, I could break it down for the students.

That was what made a good professor.

I slid the shiny new statistics textbook toward me and opened it to the first page.

Something was wrong with me. Anytime I opened a new textbook, I got a little thrill of anticipation.

Even with statistics.

It wouldn't last long, but I enjoyed it while it lasted.

The first thing I had to do was to map out the semester. Plan when I'd cover each chapter. Each test.

This was one of my superpowers.

I did this part on a yellow legal pad.

I grabbed my phone for the calendar.

But before I opened up the calendar, my fingers hovered over the text my sister had sent me yesterday.

I hadn't opened it.

I'm not sure where I got such strong willpower, but it didn't matter. I'd used it all up.

My willpower was depleted.

I opened up my sister's text and downloaded the photo of Theodore into my phone.

Taking a deep breath, I opened up the photo and studied it.

I had nothing against baseball, but I couldn't call myself a big fan, so it was not surprising that I didn't recognize the uniform he wore.

He looked a little older than he'd looked in high school, but the picture could have been taken any time between then and now.

That was the thing about dating apps. People had a tendency to put their best photos on there even if they weren't exactly up to date.

He was twenty-eight-years-old. It was possible he hadn't aged well.

I'd run into another guy who was our age at the Piggly Wiggly last week. John. He'd been in our class, but I hadn't recognized him until he said something to me. He still worked at the lumberyard where he'd worked in high school and he'd gained at least twenty pounds since. I would have taken him for a man in his mid-thirties.

So not everyone seemed to age at the same rate.

Since Theodore had shown up on Zoe's dating app, did that mean he lived in Houston? I hadn't asked her what parameters she'd put in for location.

I would ask her. Later. Maybe.

Staring at my ex-boyfriend's photograph wasn't getting any work done.

Grandma would be getting up soon and I would have to make her some breakfast. She liked cheesy eggs and bacon on toast. It only took me a few minutes to make, but I really wanted to get some stats read beforehand.

But first I got up to pour my second cup of coffee.

It was Zoe's fault. I had been doing just fine not thinking about Theodore.

I'd been doing just perfectly fine.

$$\mathcal{Chapter\ Six}$$

THEODORE

Home for the holidays.

It was always an adventure of one sort or another.

I stood on the runway that passed for an airport just west of my hometown of Maple Creek.

Low hanging clouds were coming in as predicted.

I'd just gotten back from taking the Aston Martin Airbus parked behind me up for a spin. The luxury helicopter was low mileage. A steal in my opinion. My brother-in-law, James, was thinking about buying it and wanted my opinion.

While my two older brothers and one of my brothers-in-law were airplane pilots, my newest brother-in-law flew both airplanes and helicopters.

They all flew for the same company. Skye Travels. Skye Travels had been founded by a man who was legendary in the field of avia-tion—Noah Worthington.

Noah Worthington had started off with one little Cessna airplane and had quickly grown it into the most successful private airline company in the country. He had airplanes housed in all sorts of places, mostly small towns, like Whiskey Springs in Colorado and Mackinac Island in Michigan.

His company was the one all the graduating pilots lined up to apply to work for.

Like my brothers, I had jet fuel running through my blood, but I had gone a slightly different route. While they were busy flying airplanes, I was off doing my own thing.

I did not want to be tied down. My sister, Genevieve and her husband lived in Houston, but the rest of my family lived right here in Maple Creek.

I had other ideas.

Those other ideas were part of why I had come home early for Christmas this year. I wanted to talk to my family.

I already knew how they were going to react. It was not going to be pretty.

Everyone always took my older brother, Jonathan, as my parents' favorite child, but as the youngest boy, I knew that wasn't particularly true.

Being the youngest in the family was a hard mold to break out of.

Once the youngest child, it seemed, always the youngest child.

I checked my phone. James, the keeper of this particular aircraft was supposed to be here any minute to give me a ride back to my parents' house.

I pulled my coat closer and wondered why I hadn't driven myself.

Despite being the one everyone in the family tried to look out for, I was actually the most self-sufficient. Part of that self-sufficiency meant I took care of myself.

While I'd been training to fly helicopters out in Austin, I had made some very interesting contacts. A lot of success really was about who a person knew as much as his ability and perseverance.

I had all of those and now I knew people. People who could not be met in Maple Creek.

And now I had offers.

Offers that would be hard to turn down.

A man did not become successful by sitting back and working for the man. Even if that man was Noah Worthington of Skye Travels.

An old blue truck turned into the airport and I started walking away from the helicopter.

After putting the truck in park, James opened the door and stepped out.

"Well," he said. "What do you think?"

"I think it's just fine," I said. "You can't go wrong with it."

"Hop in," James said. "Let's head home. I want to talk to you about something."

I climbed into the old truck and closed the squeaky door.

One of the things I'd learned about myself while I was in Austin was that I did not want to get stuck here in Maple Creek, riding around in an old truck from the last century.

I was a modern guy and I wanted modern things.

I wanted more.

It didn't seem like too much to ask.

I fastened the seat belt, what there was of it—no shoulder harness—and James headed out toward the highway.

"What did you want to talk to me about?"

"Jumping right to the chase?" he asked. "Alright. I want to make you an offer."

I cringed, but since James lived in Houston, not Maple Creek, I'd hear him out. There could be something to what he was going to ask me.

My grandfather had taught me a thing or two about making investments and I had found ways to implement them.

Even though I had been young, probably much too young to be learning about things like investments, it seemed, as far as I could tell, that I was the only person in the family who actually listened to what he had to teach.

I was good at it, too.

I was good at two things. Investments and flying helicopters.

As far as I was concerned, those two things were enough to make me successful.

The old truck jerked and hiccupped as James pulled out onto the highway.

Why people insisted on driving this old truck was beyond me.

I had a BMW that was so much more comfortable and so much safer than this truck, it didn't even compare.

"Tell me about the offer," I said, but I was already ninety percent sure I wasn't going to take it.

Grandpa had taught me to never disregard that ten percent. That ten percent might just be hiding a hidden gem of possibilities.

"Since we're the only two people who fly helicopters around here," he said. "I was thinking we could start our own company."

"By here you mean Maple Creek?"

"Maple Creek. Houston. The general area."

"Trying to compete with the boss?" I asked.

"Oh no. Absolutely not. Where do you think I'm getting the investment for the Aston Martin?"

"I don't understand," I said. "I thought you said you were going into business."

"We'll look over some of the numbers when we get home," he said. "You might be surprised."

Yes. I might be surprised. I had to remember to keep an open mind.

There might be something I could do to help out the family before I went off on my next venture.

That was one of the good things about being part of such a large family. It was easy to find ways to fly under the radar, especially since I didn't live here.

Unfortunately for James, I had a few other pieces of business to take care of while I was here. Some of them business. One of them personal.

The one that was personal was one that I had been putting off for far too long.

I'd tried calling her once. I'd try again soon.

In fact, maybe it was time to try something a little more direct.

Chapter Seven

While my grandmother was out walking with Doreen, I took advantage of the break and went into town to pick up a couple of things from the General Store.

Mostly it was just an excuse to get out and take a walk by myself.

The air was fresh with winter's chill and the scent of wood smoke wafting from the neighbor's chimney.

The cold weather added to the feeling of Christmastime.

Even in mid-morning, the town sparkled with Christmas lights. Shoppers were already out, looking for that perfect gift with only days to go before Christmas.

Speaking of perfect gifts, I'd come back from Houston yesterday empty-handed. That never happened to me.

It was Zoe's fault. I'd been making some progress on my shopping ideas until she showed me Theodore's photo on a dating app.

I should feel some consolation that he was on a dating app. Him being on a dating app meant he was still single. And yet somehow thinking about him dating others didn't set well with me.

In fact, I didn't like the idea of him looking for someone to date at all.

Annoyed with the direction of my thoughts, I ducked into the corner coffee shop for a coffee.

Besides smelling like rich aromatic coffee, it smelled like vanilla, caramel, and peppermint.

The roar of the coffee grinder and the hum of the expresso machine overshadowed the cheerful Christmas music spilling from the speakers.

A line of people waited to place their orders and another line of people waited to pick up their orders.

I seriously considered turning around and walking out. I'd already had two cups of coffee at home.

But I liked being in the coffee shop. It had a cozy, yet urban feel to it. It reminded me, almost, of being in Houston.

The people, though, were dressed different than the typical customer in Houston. The Maple Creek customer was more casual. The guys mostly wore jeans and flannel shirts, except for the vice-president of the bank who walked in wearing a suit.

I realized that I fit right in. I was wearing jeans and a sweatshirt beneath my long wool coat. The problem was I didn't *feel* like I fit in.

It was interesting to me that my sister and I had been raised in the same house with the same cats with the same parents. And yet we were so different.

She was content to live here in Maple Creek and work in the bakery. Granted, the owner had taken her under her wing and Zoe was becoming quite the baker. Still. It was a small bakery in Maple Creek.

I had moved here to take care of my grandmother, but I didn't see myself living here forever.

The guy I had dated last year had lived in Houston. It was only after he had broken up with me that I had decided to move in with my grandmother.

I didn't know if I would have moved here if he and I were still together. That was one of those things I would probably never have an answer for.

When I reached the counter, the young barista smiled at me. According to his name tag, his name was Eric.

"What can I get for you Dr. Flynn?"

I blinked, surprised that he knew my name.

"A small vanilla cappuccino with caramel."

"Yes ma'am." He entered the order in the computer.

"How do you know my name?" I asked.

"I'm in your class." Eric grinned.

"Is that so? Which one?"

"Introduction to Psychology," he said. "I really like it. I'm thinking about changing my major to psychology."

"Really? What do you want to do?"

He looked blankly at me.

I expected the usual answer. The one students almost always gave me. *I want to help people.*

I'd done the same thing, but I now knew that people might *go* into psychology to help people, but they didn't *stay* in psychology for the same reason.

"I want to do research," he said. "I want to understand why people do what they do."

"That a good reason," I said surprised. "Do you like math?"

"I love math. I won state championship in math my senior year. I'm taking statistics next term. I can't wait."

"I don't think I've ever heard a student say that they were excited about taking statistics. I'm going to be teaching it in spring."

"Awesome," he said. "I'll take your class."

I swiped my card and moved aside.

"I'll see you in class then."

"Sounds good," Eric said. "Your coffee will be right out."

Wondering how it was possible that I had stumbled across not only one of my online students, but one who was actually looking forward to taking statistics, I turned and nearly bumped into someone.

"Still charming young classmates?" that someone asked.

I froze right there.

I knew that voice like I knew the voice in my own head.

With my heart still pounding so fast, I couldn't think, I looked up into oh so familiar bluest of blue eyes smiling at me.

"Theodore," I breathed.

"Hello Emma."

"Hi."

Lightly taking my elbow, he steered me out of the way of other customers waiting for their coffee.

"I didn't know you were still in school," he said.

"I'm not in school," I said, finally finding my voice.

"I guess I misunderstood young Eric there."

"Eric?"

"The barista."

"Right." I glanced quickly over my shoulder. I'd all but forgotten that I had even been talking to Eric.

"I'm his professor," I said.

"Ah. That makes a whole lot more sense."

"Are you... getting coffee?"

"I don't know. Maybe."

"But you're here," I said, amused. "In the coffee shop."

"Yeah." He put his hands in his pockets and, straightening, quickly scanned the coffee shop, then his gaze landed back on mine.

"I like coffee shops," he said.

I nodded slowly, feeling the sensation of heat rising in my cheeks.

There was so much meaning in those four words and hearing him say them warmed me from the inside out.

I forgot that I hadn't seen him in ten years.

I forgot that he had broken my heart.

I forgot that he was looking to date others.

All I remembered in that moment was that he and I had met in a coffee shop.

This coffee shop to be exact.

Chapter Eight

I was sitting with my younger sister, Zoe in the town's coffee shop.

It was the week before Christmas and our parents had left us here while they went down the street to do some shopping. They had left us with strict instructions that we could drink all the hot chocolate we wanted.

I was in charge of Zoe who although she was only two years younger than me, was acting like a child. A very bad child.

"Let's get coffee," Zoe said, looking around, her blonde pony-tail swinging.

"Mom and Dad said we could have hot chocolate. Not coffee."

"They don't have to know."

I stared at my sister. We might be sisters, but we were polar opposites in so many ways.

She was blonde. I had dark brunette hair.

She was always pushing the limits. I was the good girl. If our parents told us not to drink coffee, then I wouldn't drink coffee.

Zoe, on the other hand, wanted coffee simply because it was off-limits.

A group of three guys walked in the door, snagging our attention away from our conversation.

"Who are they?" Zoe asked.

"I don't know," I said with all the nonchalance of a fifteen-year-old girl. But it didn't keep me from watching them and it certainly didn't keep me from appreciating that they did not look like they were from Maple Creek.

That was always a plus in my book.

"The one wearing the black jacket looks familiar."

"They're all wearing black coats," I said, absently.

"The leather jacket," Zoe said crossly. "He looks familiar."

I shook my head. "I don't think so."

"Give me the credit card," Zoe said, holding out her hand.

"Why?" I asked suspiciously.

"I'm going to buy another cup of hot chocolate," Zoe said sweetly.

I didn't trust her, not really, but I gave her the credit card anyway.

"While I'm there, I'll find out who they are," Zoe said as she stood up.

"No," I said, but it was to no avail. Zoe was already in line behind them.

When they turned, Zoe smiled.

She was only thirteen, but had a way of charming people that I envied.

While Zoe talked, the youngest one, the one in the leather jacket that Zoe had said looked familiar, caught my gaze and smiled.

My heart turned over and landed back where it started, but it wasn't quite in the same place it had been before. It felt a little off-kilter. So much so that I had a feeling it would never be the same again.

The guy was my age. He'd seemed older when he first walked in with the two other guys, both older.

But now I could see that he was younger than they were.

He was cute and I immediately liked him.

Zoe looked over her shoulder and I heard her say "that's my sister."

Please don't embarrass me, Zoe.

The leather jacket guy, ignoring Zoe, left the other two guys and started walking toward me.

I looked away, feeling like I'd been busted staring at him.

There was no need for him to come in this direction. The door was behind him. Everything was behind him.

He reached my table and stopped.

Looking up, I gazed into the bluest eyes I had ever seen.

"Hi," he said.

"Hi."

"I'm Theodore. Can I sit here?"

"My sister..." I looked up toward where my sister stood in line behind his companions. Then turning my gaze back to him, I nodded. "Okay."

"You're Emma," he said.

"How do you know that?"

"Your sister…"

I was going to kill her.

"Are you getting coffee?" I asked, wanting him to think that I wanted him to leave.

But I didn't want him to leave.

"Maybe," he said. "I just came in here with my brothers."

"Brothers." I looked briefly at the other two boys, then back to Theodore. "You don't look so much like them."

"Thank you."

I smiled nervously.

"Your sister," he said.

"No," I said, shaking my head. "I've never seen her before."

He laughed out loud. "The two of you are definitely sisters. You look alike."

"Really?" I asked. "No one has ever told me that before."

"What? That you look alike?"

"Everyone says we look like opposites."

"Opposite sides of the same coin." He grinned.

"Huh."

"Do you go to school here in Maple Creek?"

"Yes," I said with a little wrinkle of my nose.

"What? You don't like it?"

"It's Maple Creek. Not much to like."

"Well. I'm going to be finding out."

"What do you mean?" I didn't try to think about what he meant.

"I'm transferring here starting next month."

"Transferring from where? Where are you from?"

"Oh. I'm from here. but I've been in boarding school."

"Boarding school? Isn't that where they send troublemakers?"

"I think you're thinking of boot camp. Different places."

"I've never known anyone who went to boarding school."

"Yes. Well. I was supposed to graduate there, but my parents suddenly decided I needed to come home for high school."

"Why?" I asked.

"Parents," he said with a little shrug.

"Oh. Right." I understood completely. It was the only explanation for a whole lot of things.

"You wouldn't happen to be in the ninth grade, would you?" he asked.

"I am in ninth grade."

"Yeah? Well. Maybe you can show me around."

"Sure. I can do that," I said, trying to sound like it was no big deal.

But on the inside I was quivering with emotions I couldn't even begin to explain.

Theodore, coming in from boarding school, whatever that was, was going to be the most handsome guy in our school. Easily. Hands down.

And he wanted me to show him around.

Life in Maple Creek had just gotten a whole lot more interesting.

Chapter Nine

Theodore

James wanted to talk to me about business, so he'd parked his old truck right there on the side of the street in front of the coffee shop. I'd have at least parked it around the corner out of sight.

But this was Maple Creek and no one thought anything about an old rusty truck. If I didn't know better, I'd appreciate the lack of judgement, but being from here, I knew that wasn't the case. There was plenty of judgement to go around. Unfortunately, it was simply acceptance. The Devereaux's old truck was simply something that had always been here. It was as much a part of the town as the wooden boxes of ivies along the sidewalk and the thousands of strings of colorfully twinkling Christmas lights draped everywhere.

While James talked to his wife—my sister—on the phone, I'd gone up to order him a coffee.

And that's when I'd seen her.

Emma Flynn.

The girl I had left behind.

Ambitious to a fault, I hadn't been willing to let anything hold me back.

I'd gotten accepted into Auburn University, one of the best aviation colleges in the country.

Unfortunately, I had been so focused on that, I had been careless with Emma.

Being careless with her was by far my biggest regret in life.

She hadn't deserved to be treated the way I'd treated her. She'd been nothing but good to me.

I could have handled things so much differently. I could have given her the option to go to Auburn with me. Or we could have maintained a long-distance relationship until we figured out how to be together again.

Not that I was a fan of long-distance relationships, but if anyone could do it, she and I could have. Besides, that's what pilots did. Pilots didn't let living in a different state keep them from their girl.

She and I had been perfectly matched.

In fact, over the last nearly ten years since, I had automatically compared every girl I met to Emma.

Every single one of them came up short.

If not for Emma, I would probably have been married by now. But every girl I met quite simply just *wasn't Emma.*

That became my bottom line and I had given up.

Now that I was thinking about leaving Texas, I needed to put her behind me. I needed to see her. To get closure. With any luck, she would be married with a passel of kids. Or maybe she would have changed and I would no longer be attracted to her.

It would have been a good way to settle my mind and move on.

But. No.

The Emma that stood next to me had grown up into a beautiful young lady. If anything, she was even more beautiful than the pretty girl I'd dated in high school.

Getting closure with her was going to be harder than I had planned.

Standing here with her, I was reminded of the day we had met. Right here in this coffee shop.

Since that day, coffee shops had held a special place in my heart.

Every time I stepped inside one, I thought of Emma. And every time I came into this coffee shop in Maple Creek, I not only thought of Emma, I actually looked for her. I looked across the room at the table where I had first seen her.

She was never there, of course.

I'd lost track of her after I left her. She'd left Maple Creek, too, and had gone under the gossip radar.

Either she wasn't big on social media or she had changed her name or she was good at hiding.

Beneath the scent of coffee and vanilla of the coffee shop, I caught a whiff of her familiar scent. Lavender.

The scent brought back a wave of memories.

I'd thought about her a lot over the years, but standing here next to her, smelling the lavender scent she still wore, a whole host of long buried memories came to the surface.

Like all the afternoons we'd sat here doing our homework. Hours spent quizzing each other on history and biology.

Christmases like this one where we had taken a break from shopping in the little stores along Main Street.

"Why are you here?" Emma asked, tucking her hair in what I recognized as a nervous gesture, behind an ear.

"My brother-in-law," I said.

She looked behind me until she spotted James pacing up and down Main Street.

"I thought he and Genevieve lived in Houston," she said, her brow furrowed.

"They do. But they're here for Christmas."

"Right," she said, returning her gaze to mine.

I fell into her deep green eyes. What was it about a girl with green eyes? She was like a siren luring me onto the rocks. I was helpless against those green eyes.

How was it I'd been all over the country and I'd never come across another girl with green eyes like Emma's?

Most of the girls I'd dated had been blonde with blue eyes.

Maybe I'd dated them precisely because they didn't remind me of Emma.

"You're not a baseball player," she said, softly, with a glance at my pilot's uniform.

"No. Why would you think that?" I asked.

"I don't know," she said quickly. "Something someone said."

"I used to coach little league, but that was long time ago."

"Little league," she said with perplexed and relieved expression on her face.

James disconnected his phone and headed back inside the coffee shop.

"Are you at your grandmother's?" he asked.

"Yes. I'm taking care of her."

"Oh. I hope she's well."

"She's okay. Just getting older and a little forgetful."

"I'm sorry."

James was off the phone and back at his table.

"I should get his coffee..." I stepped past her to pick up my brother's coffee. "Do you want to...?"

She lifted an eyebrow at me.

"To...?"

This was not the time to be shy. I'd planned on talking to her anyway.

"Do you want to get pizza later? Catch up?"

"Sure," she said. "But..."

My heart sank. She was going to tell me she couldn't. That she was in a relationship. That she had moved on. Didn't want to talk to me.

"I have to see if my sister can stay with our grandmother."

"Zoe's in town?"

"Zoe never left."

At least her attitude about Maple Creek hadn't changed. I had been afraid that she had accepted life in Maple Creek and was content to live out her life here.

"Don't do that," I said. "Why don't I just come there? I'll bring enough for all of us."

Tilting her head to one side, she seemed to consider.

"Okay," she said.

Chapter Ten

Emma

I had halfway planned on sitting in the coffee shop for at least a few minutes to drink my coffee, but I changed my mind and left with it instead.

Theodore was there with his brother-in-law James. I knew of James, though I hadn't actually met him. He was married to Theodore's older sister.

But if I stayed in the coffee shop, I would be too tempted to just watch Theodore.

That couldn't possibly be healthy.

I stopped and leaned against one of the cast iron lampposts with twinkly green garland wrapped around it like stripes on a candy cane.

I'd agreed to let Theodore bring pizza over tonight.

What had I been thinking?

I took a sip of the hot coffee as people walked past me, talking, laughing. Doing what people did on a Wednesday morning before Christmas.

The music changed to something more melancholy. I was familiar with the melancholy side of Christmas to be sure.

Not a Christmas had passed that I hadn't had a moment of wistful memories all leading back to Maple Creek. To the coffee shop on the corner. To Theodore.

What stroke of fate had put us back here in Maple Creek in the old coffee shop at the same exact time?

I could count on one hand the number of times I'd been in the coffee shop on the corner since I'd moved back to Maple Creek.

Even using what I knew of statistics, I couldn't calculate the astronomical odds of us ending up back in the same place at the same time.

My grandmother kept up with the town's gossip through Doreen.

The Devereauxs didn't have to be in her social circle for her to hear things.

Theodore was the only unmarried Devereaux. Everyone knew that. People didn't talk much about him, though, because they didn't know him. He'd been gone for ten years. He'd never lived in Maple Creek as an adult.

Genevieve had married James, a pilot. Rumor had it that James was a helicopter pilot. I took that rumor as someone's imagination running away with them.

The Devereauxs were well known for being airplane pilots or marrying pilots. Even Theodore.

Everyone said the Devereaux boys had jet fuel in their blood.

That jet fuel was the reason why Theodore had left Maple Creek to begin with.

When he'd been accepted to Auburn, he'd left Maple Creek so fast, he'd left the town in his dust.

I could have gone with him.

I'd even applied to the psychology undergraduate program at Auburn.

I don't even know if I would have been accepted. When he'd left without so much as asking me if I wanted to go with him, I'd withdrawn my application.

The thought of going to Auburn. Of running into him when he might be dating someone else was more than I could bear.

And now he was back in Maple Creek for the holidays.

I couldn't deny that I had considered that possibility when I had moved back, but it hadn't been more than just a fleeting thought.

My focus had been getting away from Theodore and every-thing that reminded me of him. My grandmother needing help had just happened to coincide in time.

Our parents had moved to Florida to spend their retired years on the beach, leaving Zoe and Grandma here in Maple Creek. Since I had been living in Houston, their moving hadn't affected me all that much.

Zoe lived in the house we'd grown up in, so they hadn't sold it. It was still there.

Then in the mere span of two days, Theodore's photo had shown up on Zoe's dating app and Theodore himself had shown up in our old stomping grounds.

Giving my watch a quick glance, I shoved off the cast iron post and headed home. Grandma would be home soon and I needed to be there in case she decided to do something like turn on the stove or take the car for a spin.

Most of the time she was pretty good about not doing things that were dangerous, but I didn't want the blame to be on my head when she took a notion to do something that got her hurt.

I tossed my coffee cup in a wastebasket as I walked down the sidewalk toward Grandma's house.

Sometimes I envied Zoe.

How was it that she could waltz through life without a care in the world? It was like she somehow had no worry cells.

I got them all.

I was the one who worried.

Not that it did any good.

The psychologist in me knew that worry served no purpose and certainly didn't prevent bad things from happening, but I'd accepted a long time ago that worrying was just one of my traits. There were worse traits to have.

Worry just happened to be mine.

Worrying about my grandmother was what had brought me home to Maple Creek.

And in a roundabout way, my worry was the reason I had run into Theodore in the coffee shop.

The reason Theodore was bringing pizza over tonight.

I didn't have a good feeling for why he wanted to see me.

Probably just carried away with the season. Christmas did that to people. Made them nostalgic.

But if nothing else, there was one thing I was convinced of.

Everything happened for a reason.

Chapter Eleven

Theodore

"Who was that?" James asked after I handed him his coffee and sat down across from him.

"An old friend," I said.

"Maybe you won't need that dating profile after all," he said

"What? What dating profile?"

James held up a hand. "I know nothing."

"You know something," I said, but let it drop.

I didn't want to talk about dating right now and I wasn't ready to talk about Emma. I wasn't ready to tell anyone in my family that I was having dinner with her tonight. Sort of.

It counted, I decided. Just because her grandmother was going to be there didn't make it any less significant.

Some would argue that it made it even more significant.

I knew Emma's family. I knew her parents and her grandmother. I'd known her grandfather.

But we hadn't spent much of our time with her folks. We'd spent a lot of time with my family and at the coffee shop on the corner. Mostly with my family when it came right down to it.

She'd practically been part of my family.

Everyone expected us to get married. Hell, I expected us to get married.

But that was just the expectation that everyone else imposed on us. It hadn't really been something I felt like we were moving toward. Not that I had been opposed to marrying her. We had just been so young. Just a couple of kids.

They say hindsight is twenty-twenty.

I never gave that a lot of validity. Until now.

"She's pretty," James said. "Married?"

"No. I don't think so." I hadn't asked. I had just assumed that she wasn't. I would have heard if she'd gotten married, right?

I'd best get enough pizza just in case.

"Maybe you should ask her out."

"Now you sound like my sister."

"We are married, you know," he said with a grin.

"I'm well aware. What was it you wanted to talk to me about?"

People came and went as I listened to James. I forced myself to keep an open mind.

And yet as I listened to his well thought out plan, I realized that I had already made up my mind.

I already knew what I wanted to do.

I felt bad for James. As he talked about his plans, his eyes lit up. If I hadn't already made up my mind, his enthusiasm would have been contagious.

As it was, I would have to figure out a way to invest in his idea from afar.

Staying in this area was not the direction I had planned for myself.

"So... what do you think?" James asked.

"I think you have a well-thought out plan," I said.

"But..."

"Let me think about it, okay? I have a few things in the works. So I need to figure out how they all fit together."

"Take your time," James said, even though I could see the impatience radiating off of him and the disappointment in his eyes. He was ready to get started on this new venture of his.

I understood that sentiment far too well. I was ready to get started on my venture as well.

When the door opened, the little Christmas bell tinkling overhead, I looked up to see who was coming inside.

It wasn't Emma.

The sooner I got out of Maple Creek, the sooner I could put Emma Flynn behind me and stop looking for her every time a door opened.

Chapter Twelve

Emma

I'd been in my office for two hours, a highlighter in hand, getting some good reading done in my statistics textbook while Grandma took a nap. It was late afternoon when she brought a tray with two mugs of hot tea into my office.

"I need you to drive me to the Piggly Wiggly to pick up something for us to make for dinner," Grandma said, wandering into my office and standing at the window to watch a half dozen little sparrows fluttering about the bird feeder I'd helped her hang from an iron stake just outside the window.

As the birds fluttered about, bird feed scattered everywhere. The squirrels would love it being on the ground where they could get to it easily.

I looked up from my statistics textbook where I was deep into a section on the mean, median, and mode. If the class would stay this simple, all would be well. Unfortunately, it would not. I was merely scratching the surface.

"Theodore is coming tonight and bringing pizza. Remember?"

"Oh. Theodore. Right. Theodore is your young man."

I was pretty sure she didn't remember Theodore from when we'd dated in high school. Maybe when she saw him she would remember him. We hadn't spent much time with her, so it was possible she didn't remember him.

"He's not—" I sighed and inhaled the warm steam from my mug.

The only way Grandma could make sense of why Theodore would be coming to dinner was to think that he was my boyfriend.

I'd tried to explain it to her earlier, but if she had understood, which I wasn't sure she had, she had forgotten now.

I marked my page, closed my textbook, and capped my yellow highlighter.

"What time is he coming?" she asked.

"He didn't say. Why? Did you have something planned?" I knew she didn't. If she had anything planned, I would know it.

Grandma turned and smiled at me.

"Well... When I was your age and had a beau coming to visit, I did two things."

"What two things was that?"

"First of all, I would clean up the house."

"That makes sense." I nodded. "We keep it pretty clean, but we can straighten up. What's the other thing you would do?"

Grandma sat on the reading chair near the window and looked a bit mischievous.

"I would take a nice hot bath, add some curls to my hair, and put on a pretty dress."

"Grandma," I said. "It's just pizza. It's not a date."

"Emma Flynn," Grandma said. "When a young man comes calling and goes to the trouble to bring dinner, you want to look nice for him."

Grandma tended to forget that it been last century when she had dated Grandpa. She didn't seem to realize just how different things were now.

"Why don't we straighten up some, then see how much time we have left for all that primping."

"You can make light of it if you want to," Grandma said. "But primping is how a girl catches a husband."

"Grandma."

"And don't tell me you're not trying to catch a husband," she said. "Any red-blooded American girl like yourself is trying to catch a husband. Whether she admits it or not."

On some level, I had to admit that Grandma was right.

I was a red-blooded American girl and I'd be lying to myself if I said I didn't want a husband. The only thing was I wanted a husband someday. Not necessarily right now.

But we would see.

It wasn't often I had the occasion to get dressed up for anything.

Pizza with an old boyfriend or an old beau as Grandma called him might be occasion enough to break things up a little bit.

Chapter Thirteen

THEODORE

I flew airplanes and/or helicopters every day.

And yet standing here on Emma's Grandmother's doorstep, shifting three hot pizzas from hand to another, I was nervous.

There was no other way to describe the way I was feeling.

My heart was racing and my hands trembled just a little. Enough that I noticed it as I went to press the doorbell.

I couldn't say what I expected.

I'd dated Emma for three years and we had been best friends for six months before that. Maybe it hadn't been quite six months before I'd gotten up the nerve to kiss her.

I no longer had that kind of restraint. Since then, dating a girl for six months before kissing her had become about as foreign to me as anything I could imagine when it came to dating. I couldn't remember the last time I'd gone on a first date without stealing at least one kiss.

But I'd been young and time had spread out ahead of me like an endless road. A road that had no beginning and more importantly had no end.

As far as I could comprehend back then, I would be forever young.

With all the time in the world to think about getting married and settling down, I had let my career consume me.

Maybe not so much my career as my love of airplanes. The love of airplanes came first. The career followed.

Emma's grandmother answered the door.

I handed her a little bouquet of red and white daisies with a silver ribbon tied around them.

"These are for you," I said. "How are you Grandma?"

"Oh. My." Her eyes misted for just a moment as she took the bouquet I'd picked up at the flower shop while I'd waited on the pizza.

"These are so lovely. You must be Theodore."

"Yes ma'am," I said smoothly, somehow managing to hide my surprise.

Grandma didn't recognize me. Emma hadn't prepared me for that. I'd just assumed that she would remember me.

Grandma had aged a lot in ten years. Her hair was silver and not the kind that came from a salon, although she did have a stylish short haircut.

Her polite smile told me she didn't recognize me. I might be ten years older, but I was pretty sure I hadn't aged to an unrecognizable degree.

Emma had recognized me immediately.

"Come in," Grandma said. "Emma will be down shortly."

She turned around, leaving me to close and lock the door.

I followed her into the kitchen where I slid the pizza onto the kitchen island, then helped her get a vase down from one of the top shelves in the cabinet. Apparently vases weren't used all that often here. I actually took heart from that.

That meant that Emma didn't have a string of boys bringing her flowers.

Grandma filled a vase with water, then stuck the flowers into it.

I wanted to offer to cut the ends off the stems, but they were her flowers now. If she wanted to just stuff them down into the vase, then it wasn't my business.

"Let's go into the parlor and wait for Emma," Grandma said, leaving the vase of flowers near the boxes of pizza.

We retraced our steps, heading into what she called the parlor and I sat on the couch next to her.

Three stockings hung from the mantle with names embroidered on them.

Emma. Zoe. Grandma.

Garland with little red berries was draped across the top and fell on either side of the mantle.

Although there was a stack of wood next to the fireplace, the hearth was cold.

It seemed to me like it was a perfect night to have a cozy fire, especially with it being just a few days until Christmas.

"Do you want me to light a fire in the fireplace?" I asked.

"That would be lovely, Dear," she said. "Just lovely."

Kneeling in front of the fireplace, I carefully arranged the logs, then used the lighter to start the fire.

I was working on it, nurturing the little flame when Emma came to stand beside me. I knew it was her before she even spoke.

"Has Grandma put you to work already?" she asked.

"I offered," I said. "It seemed like a good night to have a cozy fi —." Looking up at her, I forgot what I was saying.

Emma looked down at me with an amused smile.

Her long loosely curled hair framed her heart shaped face. She was wearing glittery lip gloss on her plump full lips and her green eyes were framed with thick lashes.

She was wearing an emerald green velvet dress that hugged her in all the right places and hung loose in the others. She was wearing sparkly silver heels.

Not what I would have thought a Maple Creek girl would wear to a casual pizza dinner in her own home.

She could have easily passed for a casual night out in Houston or any other city for that matter.

"Hi," she said.

"Hi." I looked over my shoulder for her grandmother, but Grandma had quietly vanished.

"Grandma went to get the pizza."

"I could have brought it," I said. "I just assumed we'd eat in the... um..."

"Kitchen?"

"Yes. Kitchen. Why are you all dressed up?"

"Dressed up? This old thing?" She ran a hand down the length of her dress, making my throat go dry.

"I brought pizza. And plates," Grandma said, coming into the parlor.

Emma smiled at me and turned away.

"Doesn't she look adorable?" Grandma said, setting everything down on the coffee table.

"Grandma," Emma said, blushing prettily.

I grinned at Emma.

Just a minute ago, she was flirting with me and now she looked shy. All in the span of a minute.

I couldn't make sense of it. Flirty one second. Shy the next.

Had she always been this way?

She could have been and I probably wouldn't even have noticed it. As a teenager, I must have been terribly self-absorbed to not have noticed these things about Emma.

Now, as I was nearing thirty and I'd been out in the world, I noticed things I hadn't noticed before.

Grandma sat on the chair while Emma and I sat on the sofa.

"You brought a lot of pizza," Emma said as she lifted the lids on the pizza boxes.

"I didn't know how many people would be joining us."

Ignoring my comment, her face lit up with surprise and she turned to me.

"You brought black olive and pineapple."

"You're the only person I've ever known who likes a black olive and pineapple pizza."

"I guess that would be hard to forget," she said, looking at me with her mesmerizing green eyes.

"Very hard to forget," I said. I didn't think we were talking about pizza anymore. I wasn't. I was talking about her. It would have been impossible for me to forget about Emma.

I might have missed... or maybe forgotten... a few of her nuances, but I remembered little things. Like what kind of pizza she liked. Like the excitement on her face when she beat me at a card game. Even if she hadn't won fair and square, I would have let her win just to see the triumph on her face.

I remembered the way she closed her eyes and sighed when my lips touched hers.

"I'll be right back," Emma said, standing up. "Do you want water or soda?"

"Water is fine," I said. "But I can get it."

"No. No. I'll be right back." She vanished to the kitchen, leaving me sitting alone with Grandma.

Grandma sat with her hands clasped, studying me.

"You look familiar," she said.

"Yes, ma'am. I dated your granddaughter in high school."

Grandma smiled.

"And now you've come back," she said. "That's very romantic."

I didn't tell her why I was here.

I didn't tell her that I hadn't come here to rekindle my old romance with Emma.

And I certainly didn't tell her that sometimes no matter how hard we tried, old flames rekindled themselves spontaneously.

Chapter Fourteen

EMMA

I stood at the refrigerator door, my hand on the cool handle.

I'd needed to take a moment. Just a moment. To clear my head.

Grandma had talked me into wearing the dress I'd worn to a party last year with Edward. It had just been hanging in my closet ever since and even though I didn't anticipate wearing it anywhere else, I liked it enough to keep it.

So I'd worn it tonight at Grandma's urging.

It had seemed like harmless fun until Grandma had pointed it out to Theodore.

I'd seen the look in his eyes and it had quite honestly frightened me.

I had no reason to think that he was here for any reason other than to be friendly. For old time's sake. Or something like that.

He wasn't here to pick up where we had left off.

Too much water had passed under the bridge.

He had his life. His career. And I had mine.

Not only that, I had my grandmother to take care of.

Pulling three bottles of cold water out of the refrigerator, I made my way back into the parlor.

Theodore and Grandma were talking like old friends.

Theodore was like that. He could talk to anyone about anything.

It was part of his charm.

Going back to the sofa, I sat down next to Theodore and handed each of them a bottle of water.

"Your grandmother was just telling me that your parents moved to Florida."

"They did."

"I didn't think they would ever leave Maple Creek."

"I guess I didn't either. Zoe lives in their house now." I opened my water and took a sip.

"I see. So they left themselves an option to come back."

"I hadn't thought of it like that. But I guess they did. Zoe might protest if they tried that. She's made the house her own."

"Sometimes it's comforting just to know there's an option to come back to something familiar. Even if we don't do it."

I looked at him sideways.

I couldn't tell if he was talking about my parents now or if he was talking about himself. Was he saying he liked having the option to come back even if he didn't do it?

"Let's not let this pizza get cold," Grandma said.

"Right." I handed her a plate, then handed one to Theodore. "Help yourself."

"Ladies first," Theodore said.

Once a gentleman, always a gentleman.

It was good to know that some things never changed.

I put a slice of pineapple and black olive pizza on my plate—still my favorite, then waited for Theodore to grab a slice of pepperoni.

The fire in the hearth had taken hold and blazed up, creating a comfortable, cozy atmosphere.

The six-foot artificial Christmas tree Grandma and I had decorated with yards of bright twinkling lights and hundreds of decorations she had collected over the years brought back bittersweet memories.

Somehow those memories of days gone by hadn't bothered me so much when I'd felt like I was moving forward.

Now I felt like I had come full circle and that made me sad.

As I watched Theodore from beneath my lashes, the things I had left behind—Theodore specifically—suddenly seemed all that much more important.

I suddenly felt a chasm of regret about what felt like lost years.

He'd been the one to break up with me, but that hadn't stopped me from comparing every guy I ever dated to him.

It hadn't stopped me from missing him.

And it certainly hadn't stopped me from loving him.

$$Chapter\ Fifteen$$

The lights on the artificial Christmas tree twinkled red and blue and green. I couldn't remember ever seeing quite so many ornaments on one tree. Most of them were obviously very old.

We had two trees at our house now. We had one in the kitchen with some of our older decorations and we had one in our living room that I thought of as the showpiece. It was the one people saw when they drove up our circle drive and the one they saw when they stepped inside our front door.

There was something charmingly cozy about the tree in Grandma's living room. I guess technically it was also Emma's living room since she was living here with Grandma.

I couldn't help wondering what kind of tree Emma would

have if the decorations had been up to her. I had a feeling she had acquiesced to Grandma's style.

I poked at the little fire I'd started, adjusted the logs, added fresh cut logs sending embers up the chimney.

After we ate, Grandma excused herself, saying she'd had a long day.

I didn't miss the look she exchanged with Emma as she left us, heading to her bedroom. Even though I had sisters, there were still certain looks, like that one, that I couldn't interpret.

"How long have you been working from home?" I asked.

"For a while now. I was actually hired as a remote professor."

"Remote professor. Who would have thought? Do you like it?" I asked.

"It allows me to be here to help Grandma out."

That didn't exactly answer my question, but I let it go for now. I wondered just how much of herself she had given up in order to be Grandma's caregiver.

"She doesn't remember me," I said.

"I know." Emma sighed. "You have to remember that it's been ten years and we didn't spend a lot of time around her back then."

"If I remember correctly, she and your grandfather were doing a lot of traveling."

"You're right. They did. They had one of those motor homes."

"I can't imagine traveling that way. I like to get where I'm going."

"I think they liked the trip as well as the destination."

"What about you?" I asked, kneeling in front of the fireplace again to poke at the logs.

"What about me what?"

"Have you had the chance to travel much? Or can you live without it?"

She slipped off one of her shoes and stared into the flames.

"I lived in Houston until a few months ago when I moved back to Maple Creek. Other than that, I haven't traveled much."

"Do you miss it? Houston?"

"I miss it some."

I dusted off my hands and went to sit back on the sofa next to her.

"Here," I said, motioning toward her feet.

"What?"

"Give me your feet."

"Theodore. You can't just—"

I shrugged. "I guess you don't like to have your feet rubbed anymore."

"I like it fine," she said with a bit of annoyance.

I sat back and waited.

"Fine," she said, kicking off her other shoe and adjusting her dress and turning so that she could put her feet in my lap.

I started with her toes and worked my way along the soles of her feet.

When she closed her eyes and let out a little sigh, I smiled to myself.

"Where did you learn to do that?" she asked.

"I actually took a class."

"You did not," she said with a half-hearted protest.

"I have the certificate to prove it."

"Is there nothing you can't do?" she asked, sleepily.

I decided the question was rhetorical and she didn't really want an answer. So I didn't answer.

I just enjoyed the moment and let her do the same.

A car passed slowly along the street outside and a dog barked somewhere in someone's back yard. Another dog in another back yard answered.

Such was life in the small town.

A lot of things might may have changed, but there were a lot of things that hadn't.

It was good to know that my girl still liked her feet massaged.

Chapter Sixteen

With the Christmas tree lights flickering in the low light and the glow of the flames in the fireplace, I took a little trip back in time.

Theodore had always had a knack for massages. I could, in fact, say that he had learned on me, but he'd taken classes since and I could tell. His fingers moved with skill that only came from training.

He still had the gentleness that he'd had before. He just seemed to know more about what he was doing.

"You don't have a boyfriend?" he asked as he massaged the tension out of my feet.

"Not anymore," I said.

"Oh. I'm sorry."

"No need to apologize." I opened my eyes and looked at him. "Turns out it was for the best."

"I can relate to that."

"What about you? Do you have a girlfriend? No. Wait. Maybe you shouldn't answer that right now."

"Why not?" He moved to her other foot.

"Because if you tell me you have a girlfriend, I'll have to make you stop."

"So you're okay with me massaging your feet as long as you don't know about my girlfriend."

I tugged at my foot, my eyes widening.

"Stop it," he said. "I don't have a girlfriend. You know me better than that."

"Maybe you changed." But she relaxed again, closing her eyes.

"You're the psychologist. Do people change that much?"

"Not usually."

"Not usually. But sometimes?"

"Maybe. I can't think right now."

"It's good to know I still have that effect on you." It was meant teasingly, but something told me he meant every word.

I opened my eyes enough to give him a look.

"You haven't changed. You're still incorrigible."

"You wouldn't have it any other way."

"You're funny. Shouldn't you be with your family?"

"Why?" he asked. "They're all married."

"That doesn't mean anything."

"They're okay without me."

Sometimes I didn't understand Theodore. He had a big loving family and he didn't feel compelled to spend time with them.

"You don't think they miss you?" I asked.

"Not really," he said. "They're all content doing their own thing."

"You are truly a youngest child."

He ran a finger lightly along the bottom of my foot.

"Hey," I said, tugging at my foot. "No tickling."

"Just trying to live up to my reputation of being the youngest child."

I studied him then. The boy had grown into a man. And yet when I looked at him, at the moment at least, I saw more of the boy than the man.

He was the same. Yet different.

Chapter Seventeen

Emma and I talked until nearly Midnight. I'd burned up the bundle of firewood that had been stacked by the hearth and now the fire burned low.

It was time for me to go home.

I found that I didn't want to leave her even though I was just driving across town.

"Walk me to the door," I said. "I know you have things you have to do tomorrow and you need your beauty sleep."

"It was good to see you," she said, leaving her shoes off as we walked to the door. "And it was nice to catch up."

"It was."

I couldn't tell her I wanted to see her again and I wasn't one of those guys who said they would call when they knew they weren't going to.

And yet I hadn't done what I had come here to do. I had come here to tell her I was going away. I had come here to put her behind me.

Instead of putting her behind me, though, I had found that the pretty girl I had loved when we were teenagers had grown into an even more beautiful woman.

That wasn't supposed to happen.

Seeing her was supposed to help me put my feelings behind, not bring them back to the surface.

Unfortunately, spending the evening with her had quite simply felt right.

It wasn't supposed to feel right.

What was it supposed to feel like anyway?

We reached the door and I looked at her with all the intent in the world to tell her that I had decided to go away.

But she looked so relaxed. So content.

So sweet.

I couldn't do it.

I couldn't tell her. Not now.

I'd tell her tomorrow.

Reaching out to tuck a strand of hair behind her ear, an old gesture that apparently was still automatic, I let my hand drop instead before it reached her.

"Can I buy you lunch tomorrow?" I asked.

I saw a flash of something unrecognizable cross her features. Something that struck me deep in my heart. It looked a lot like hope.

"Sure," she said with a little shrug. "Okay."

"Good," I said. "I'll come by around one o'clock. Pick you up."

Without her shoes, Emma looked irresistibly dainty and petite. I had forgotten I was a full head taller than her. Or maybe I had grown a bit taller since high school.

I needed to leave now. Before I started something I couldn't finish.

"I'll see you tomorrow then," I said, opening the door.

"Be safe," she said.

I reached my car quickly. Even as I got into the driver's seat, I knew she stood at the door and watched me.

She was still standing there, watching me as I backed out of the driveway and drove down the street.

I knew because I watched her in my rear view mirror.

Reaching Main Street, I turned right. The town still twinkled with festively colored Christmas lights.

It had been ten years since I'd been with Emma at Christmas-time and yet it seemed like all the other years, the ones when I hadn't been with her, just folded in like an accordion and weren't worth remembering or even thinking about.

I had to get myself together. I was going away.

I couldn't do anything to make Emma think that we could pick up where we had left off.

I had hurt her once. I wouldn't do it again.

But it wasn't just Emma that I had to worry about.

I had to worry about myself. I'd spent ten years growing my regret at leaving Emma behind. Maybe I hadn't thought to regret it at first, but as the years passed, I had realized what an idiot I had been.

I couldn't do it again. I couldn't be that same idiot all over again. Leaving the girl I loved behind because I had grand plans.

By the time I turned off the highway into my family's driveway, I realized that history was repeating itself all over again.

I had big plans. Something I wanted to do.

And I was leaving Emma behind.

That was the thing about history.

Things always came back around again.

This time I had to do something differently.

I just didn't know what that something was going to be.

Chapter Eighteen

Emma

I slept in the next morning.

I knew I had overslept when I heard Grandma in the kitchen.

At first the scent of bacon and biscuits took me back to the days when I was a child and Grandma made breakfast every morning when I spent the night with her.

It only took a moment though, for that nostalgia to turn into alarm. Grandma wasn't supposed to be in the kitchen. That was a big part of why I was living here. So she didn't have to put herself in danger of burning the house down.

Still wearing my pajamas, I found her in the kitchen. Right where she wasn't supposed to be.

"Good morning," Grandma said brightly when she saw me.

"Good morning." She looked so happy, I didn't have the heart to remind her that she wasn't supposed to be in the kitchen. "What are you doing?"

"I made breakfast," she said, looking quite pleased with herself.

"It smells wonderful."

Putting a thick mitt on her hand, she pulled a pan of biscuits out of the oven.

"I was just about to come and wake you," she said. "I know you like biscuits with eggs and bacon. Extra crispy."

"Let me help you," I said. "I'll put some butter on the biscuits and make those little biscuits sandwiches out of them." Just like we used to.

"I'll get the orange juice," Grandma said. "And we can sit at the breakfast table."

I pushed aside the potted poinsettia Doreen had given Grandma that sat in the middle of the breakfast table that overlooked the backyard. In spring and summer it would burst with brightly colored flowers. Now though, in the dead of winter, there was winter grass, but no flowers. Just bare limbed maple trees.

"How was your date with your young man?" Grandma asked as I poured orange juice into two glasses.

"He's not—" She wouldn't understand. "It was nice."

Maybe I was the one who didn't understand.

Theodore had been what Grandma called *my young man* at one time. He wasn't now. At least not technically.

But wasn't it possible that he always would be in one way or another?

If I never stopped loving him, did that mean something even if we weren't together?

I didn't know how I was ever going to replace him, but I did know that I had to start figuring something out.

I had to figure it out because Theodore Devereaux did not let moss grow under his feet.

That was something anyone who knew him at all had to know.

"We're having lunch today," I blurted before I could stop myself.

"That's wonderful," Grandma said, beaming. "I just knew there was something special between the two of you."

"Maybe," I said, breaking a piece of bacon into two pieces. "But he doesn't live here, Grandma. He doesn't live in Maple Creek."

"Well. Where does he live?"

That was a good question.

"I don't know. I didn't ask him."

"Oh. Emma, dear. You have to ask him. People, men especially, like to talk about themselves."

"I know," I said. "I'll ask him today."

"Good girl. Eat up. Then we'll go see what you have in your closet to wear."

"It's just—" I said.

"Lunch. I know it's just lunch. But that's no excuse not to look your best. Back when I was your age, a girl never left the house without a skirt and matching jacket. Hair and makeup just right. It was even more important when we were meeting a beau."

"Alright, Grandma. I'll try to do it right."

After all, what did I have to lose?

It turned out I had nothing in my closet that was Grandma approved.

So at nine thirty, I found myself walking toward town with Grandma, Doreen in tow.

They were convinced that I would find the perfect outfit to wear in downtown Maple Creek. A Houston shopper, myself, I wasn't convinced that I would find anything.

Fortunately, I had jeans and a sweater on backup.

Chapter Nineteen

Emma wasn't the only person I had to break the news of my plans to.

I had to tell my whole family about my new venture that would take me away from Texas.

Fortunately, I had until after Christmas to tell them and I decided that I would do just that. I would wait until after Christmas.

It made me feel a little bit deceptive. I didn't like having made such a huge decision and not telling them.

Once I left, I was pretty sure I wouldn't be coming home much more than once a year at Christmas.

Since I hadn't told them this, they acted like nothing was different.

"Why are you being so quiet?" My sister Genevieve asked. Genevieve and I were closest in age, so out of all my siblings, I was closest to her.

Our parents had started out with one child. Jonathan. Then they'd had two more in quick succession. Waited a few years and had two more. Genevieve and I were those two youngest. It made for some interesting family dynamics.

Genevieve and I were the only two who didn't live in Maple Creek. Genevieve lived in Houston with her husband, but, of course, everyone was here for the two weeks of Christmas.

"I didn't realize I was," I said.

"You look like you're about a thousand miles away right now."

I blinked and focused on my sister. She was stirring pancake mix in a big mixing bowl.

I sat at the kitchen island, drinking my first cup of coffee and just enjoying being here with my sister.

How was it she had gotten so close to the truth?

"I guess I was just thinking," I said evasively.

"I heard you had a date with Emma last night." She turned on the griddle to get it warmed up.

"How is it even remotely possible that you know that?"

I hadn't told anyone where I was going? Had I?

"It's Maple Creek."

"Are you tracking my phone?" I asked. "Or my car?"

Genevieve laughed. "You know that's not necessary. All you have to do is drive through Main Street and someone will see you."

I stared speechlessly at her. I knew she was right. But I had been away for so long I had forgotten just how true that was.

"One of mother's friends saw your car at Emma's grandmother's house," she said. "Don't look so paranoid."

"Not paranoid. Just very frightened."

"Are you sure you're the same Theodore who grew up in Maple Creek?"

"I'm not sure I want to be."

"Well, how was it?" The first pancake sizzled as she poured it on the griddle.

"How was what?"

"Your date silly."

"It wasn't a date."

"Then... why did you take pizza over and stay until almost Midnight?"

"The neighbors really need to find something else to do."

"Actually James is the one who saw you come home late."

"I guess that's something," I muttered.

"Maybe you can bring Emma over on Christmas," Genevieve said.

"I don't think so. She has her family. Zoe and her grandmother."

Genevieve deftly poured some more drops of batter on the griddle, then flipped the first one over.

"Bring them, too," she said. "We're going to have a full house anyway."

"I don't know," I said, getting up to make myself a cappuccino on the machine someone had bought since I was here last time.

I stood watching the machine do its thing, not thinking about anything in particular.

"You're acting a little strange," Genevieve said, scooping up a pancake and smearing some butter on top. "Spit it out."

"I'm not acting strange." Much.

She tossed another pancake on top of the buttered one and slid the plate to where I was sitting.

"I'll ply you with food and you'll talk to me."

"What makes you think that will work?" I asked, sitting down and picking up a fork.

"Because men are such simple creatures." She sighed overdramatically.

The pancakes were good. As expected.

"You think since you're married, you have men figured out."

She sat down across from me and poured syrup over her own pancakes.

"I'm not sure anybody ever really figures out men." She pointed a fork at me. "But you are evading the question."

Now was about as good a time as any. If I was going to do it, I might as well just get it over with. I would tell Genevieve. Test the waters.

"I got a job offer," I blurted.

"That's good. What kind?"

"Running a private helicopter company."

Genevieve put her fork down and looked at me.

"That sounds a lot like what James is doing. But... this is something different isn't it?"

"It is. I'd still be doing some flying, but mostly supervising."

"You don't sound so sure about it?"

I smiled a little.

I was sure. At least I thought I had been sure. But I hadn't counted on just how hard it was telling my sister.

"Gen," I said. "It's in Portugal."

Genevieve looked like she was going to be sick. This was much worse than I had expected.

"Portugal? The country?"

"It's a once in a lifetime opportunity."

"I guess it is."

She gathered up her plate and took it to the sink. She didn't say anything as she tossed her no more than half eaten pancakes in the disposal.

Finally, she turned around.

"You haven't told anyone else?" she asked.

"I was going to wait until after Christmas."

"Well. I wish you hadn't told me." She looked away with a little shake of her head.

"Gen," I said. "I'm sorry."

She sat back down across from me and searched my eyes.

"James said he talked to you. Maybe he could match the deal. You wouldn't have to go."

"He can't match it," I said. "It's one of those rare offers."

"I see." She looked away. "I guess you have to do what you have to do."

"I guess we all do, don't we?"

Not looking at me, without another word, she got up and walked out of the kitchen, but not before I saw the look on her face.

The deal in Portugal really was a once in a lifetime opportunity. Not only that, but it had the potential for me to become the owner eventually.

How could I turn it down?

How could I bear the look on my sister's face if I did take it?

And if her reaction was any indication, how was I going to tell my parents?

And even worse, Emma?

Somewhere along the way, I'd started to care what Emma thought as much as I cared what my own family thought.

Chapter Twenty

Grandma and Doreen were having a blast in a little store called Hometown Threads.

They showed me several dresses, but I just shook my head. No offense to anyone in Maple Creek, but I was more of a conservative girl, especially in my style of dress.

There were lots of clothes, but all I could see were big yellow flowers and stripes and big puffy sleeves.

The manager, a new girl named Rebecca, watched in amusement as they looked at everything and tried to get me to try on something.

"Well," Grandma said, holding up a long cozy cardigan. "I'm taking this home. Don't you love it Doreen?"

"It's you. And the color is perfect. You have to get it." She picked up a sweatshirt. "I'm getting this for our walks on those cold mornings."

Rebecca came to stand next to me.

"Didn't your grandmother say they were looking for something for you?"

"They did. But it's okay. I have some jeans and a sweater I can wear."

"Do you mind if I ask the occasion?"

"It's just lunch with an old friend."

"Old boyfriend?"

I looked at her sideways.

"Sorry." She winced. "I try not to listen, but it's hard to ignore the small town talk."

"It's okay. Yes. Old boyfriend. But it's just lunch."

Rebecca nodded sagely. She wasn't much older than me, but she radiated experience.

"Most of my customers are older like your grandmother, but I'm slowly adding in some things for the younger customer. Just to see how it goes."

"I'm sure it would go well," I said. I couldn't picture anyone under thirty wearing anything in her shop.

"I have a couple of things in the back if you'd like to take a look."

"Sure," I said, not feeling particularly optimistic. It didn't make sense to have things in the back that she could be selling out front.

I followed her to the back where she took out a cutter and opened a box.

"They only just came this morning and I haven't had the chance to look at them yet."

"I see." At least that explained why she had things that weren't on display.

She emptied the box and began taking things out of packages.

"This was on backorder and it's really too late for it now." She shook out a red sweater dress. "It would have been perfect at the first of December when the holiday parties started."

"Can I see it?" I asked.

The sweater dress, in a pretty Christmas red, was as soft as it looked.

"Can I try this on?" I asked.

"Of course. I ordered this belt to go with it if you want to try it, too."

I liked Rebecca's sales style. She didn't push anything on anyone. She just let them come into her store and basically play.

As I put on the dress, then added the belt, I knew it was perfect. The three-way mirror confirmed it.

"What do you think?" I asked, stepping out of the dressing room.

"I think it's perfect," Rebecca said. "Just wear your little lace up boots, the ones you wore in, and you're all set for your date."

It's not a date.

I gave up on trying to correct people about that.

As much as people assumed it was a date, it might as well be one.

Truth be told, I didn't know what it was.

As far as I could tell, it was just a couple of old friends getting together while he was in town.

We hadn't seen each other in ten years.

He was just being polite and I was just being curious.

It wasn't a big deal.

But I wore the soft, pretty dress out of the store and it certainly felt like a big deal, especially as I listened to Doreen and Grandma talk on the walk home.

"She's got plenty of time before he comes to pick her up."

"Enough time for us to do her hair."

I'd already done my hair.

"What's wrong with my hair?"

"Nothing, Dear," Grandma said. "You just need a little more... curls. Right Doreen?"

"I can do it up in no time," Doreen said. "When Theodore sees her in that dress, he'll probably ask her to marry him right there."

Doreen might be getting a little carried away.

"I think he should take her on a proper date for that," Grandma said.

"You're so formal," Doreen said. "Let them be kids."

The two of them chattered like teenagers all the way home.

And because I was feeling a little bit excited about my date-but-not-a-date, I let Doreen do my hair.

Chapter Twenty-One

THEODORE

I walked up what was quickly becoming the familiar path to Emma's grandmother's door.

I expected Grandma to answer the door, but to my pleasant surprise, Emma opened the door.

"Hi," she said, smiling.

"Hi."

She was wearing a Christmassy red dress in something that not only looked soft to the touch, but also hugged her figure in ways that had me wondering how she'd managed to stay so fit over the last ten years.

Just like last night, she was dressed far dressier than I had expected. In fact, I felt underdressed in my jeans and sweatshirt.

"You look great," I said.

"I told Grandma it was just lunch. I can go change."

"Absolutely not," I said. "I'm the one who should go change. Besides, according to my older sister, a girl can never be over-dressed."

"Genevieve," she said. "She's a Houston girl like me."

"Yes. Yes she is. Is your grandmother okay?"

"She's over at Doreen's. We all went shopping today and now they're making lunch together."

"I'm glad she had a friend."

"Me too. Are you ready?" She grabbed her purse and tossed it over her head, then I held her wool coat while she got into it.

"Do you have any place in mind?" I asked as we walked toward my car.

"It's Maple Creek. There aren't that many options."

"I know a place. A little French restaurant."

"In Maple Creek?" She asked with appropriate skepticism.

"Hardly. In Houston."

"Oh."

"Unless you're starving, we can be there in no time on the helicopter."

"Grandma made breakfast so not starving. Helicopter?"

"Yes. I have one out at the airport."

"I've never flown in a helicopter."

"Scared?" I asked, teasingly.

"No. Maybe."

I opened the passenger door for her.

"It'll be fun," I said before I closed her door.

I'd worry about telling her my news about leaving later.

It was just a few days before Christmas.

I couldn't see any reason why I couldn't take a pretty girl to lunch in Houston... via helicopter... without ruining the magical moment by telling her I was moving to Portugal.

I got into the driver's seat and with a sudden burst of unexpected optimism, I backed out of her driveway and headed to the airport.

It was amazing how much better I felt now that I'd given myself permission to not tell her what I'd invited her to lunch to tell her.

Maybe I'd just wait.

It might be wrong to wait until after Christmas, but it seemed even more wrong to tell her now, before Christmas.

I would follow Genevieve's advice and wait to tell anyone else, including Emma.

At the moment, I was about to share my life's passion with my girl.

It seemed like a travesty that I had never taken Emma flying.

It was something long overdue as far as I was concerned.

Chapter Twenty-Two

EMMA

Flying in the helicopter with Theodore at the controls wasn't scary. At least not much.

He handled the helicopter deftly and with confidence.

I put on the extra headset and listened in on the control tower chatter.

The little town of Maple Creek disappeared below and we were on our way to Houston.

When I wasn't watching Theodore, I was looking out the window. It was different from flying in an airplane in that we weren't very high in altitude.

When the Houston skyline came into view, I straightened in my seat. We'd gotten here in no time at all and we hadn't had to fight the traffic.

"This is so much better than driving," I said.

"I know. Right? That's what I've been saying."

He flew right past the airport and headed toward uptown.

He set the helicopter down right on the roof of a building. It was absolutely cool.

"We just parked on top of a building," I said.

He laughed. "Yes we did. The French restaurant is a block from here. I hope you don't mind walking."

"I don't mind."

I didn't mind a bit. In fact, whether this was a date or not didn't matter. It was already the best date I'd ever gone on.

I took his hands to hold as I slid out of the helicopter. When I hesitated, he took me by the waist and lowered me to the ground.

Biting my lip to keep from laughing at the unexpected, I put my hands on his shoulders.

Feet on the ground now, with the blades twirling slower and slower above us, I looked up into his sparkling blue eyes. What to me were the bluest of blue eyes.

A little smile played at the corner of his lips.

"What did you think about your first helicopter ride?" he asked.

I blinked. Although he had obviously been able to think while looking into my eyes, I had to take a minute to gather my thoughts.

"I think I'm ready to trade in my car," I said.

He laughed and took my hand.

"I think you'll have to secure a pilot first."

"Surely the pilot comes with the helicopter," I said playfully.

He shook his head.

"I have so much to teach you," he said.

We walked down a flight of stairs and got onto an elevator.

"You've been here before," I said. He obviously knew his way around.

"I had to scope it out before I could bring you here."

The elevator door opened and we stepped into a deserted lobby with pristine marble floors and tall windows overlooking a well-manicured courtyard.

There was a bronze engraved directory on the wall with the names of a dozen attorneys.

It made sense now why the building would have a helipad.

"Do you have to have permission to land here?" I asked.

"Of course," he said as he opened the front door that opened out onto the busy Post Oak Boulevard.

The street was lined with hundreds of tall metal Christmas trees that would light up in a choreographed dance at sunset.

We turned right and followed the sidewalk to the corner.

When the hand turned green, we hurried across the street.

Another right turn and we stepped into an elegant little restaurant with only a dozen tables. The restaurant had no windows and the lights were low, giving it a mysterious ambiance.

We were immediately seated by a young hostess who handed us each a menu.

I leaned forward, keeping my voice low.

"My menu doesn't have any prices on it," I whispered.

"That's because you have the lady's menu."

"What's a lady's menu?"

"It's a tradition from the old days when the lady wasn't supposed to worry about how much things cost."

"How am I supposed to know what to order?"

"That's kinda the whole point. You can order whatever you want."

She looked at me a moment, her green eyes processing.

"Okay," she said finally with a little shrug. "But it won't be my fault if you have to wash dishes."

"Why am I the one who has to wash the dishes?"

"Because you're the one with the menu that has prices. Since it's obviously the man's job to pay, then it falls to the man to wash the dishes."

A server stopped by to light the candle on our table, then slipped away just as quickly.

"Hm. That's actually fair logic. And you sound eerily like my sister, Genevieve."

"I always liked Genevieve."

"She likes you, too. In fact, she suggested I invite you over for Christmas."

"Oh." There was a panic in her eyes that I couldn't quite explain. "Why would she do that? I have my grandmother and my sister."

"Your parents decided not to come home?"

"They didn't want to make the drive."

He didn't ask, but I could see the obvious question in his eyes.

"I know," I said. "They could fly."

"You'd bring them, too, of course," he said. "Your sister and your grandmother. Your parents if they were coming home."

"That's very kind of her," I said, returning my attention to my menu with no prices.

Having an invitation from his sister was kind, but it wasn't his sister who I wanted to get an invitation from.

If I was going to spend Christmas with the Devereauxs, I wanted an invitation from Theodore.

Otherwise, it meant nothing.

Chapter Twenty-Three

I'd been to this little French restaurant with my boss a long time ago. He was actually the one who had the permit to park on the roof of the nearby building, but I didn't see the need in boring Emma with the details.

Even though I'd known about this restaurant for close to three years, I'd never brought a girl here. I'd always thought it would be the perfect place for a date.

Turns out I was right.

I hadn't known they had the old-fashioned menus that didn't show the prices to the ladies, but I thought it was rather romantic.

I'd always thought it was rather crass to take a lady to a restaurant with prices sitting there on the menu.

This way, it truly felt like my treat. Maybe I was an old-fashioned guy and I hadn't even realized it.

Emma had her attention glued on the menu and I could tell something was bothering her.

I hadn't planned on telling her that Genevieve wanted me to bring Emma and her family to our house for Christmas.

I had planned on letting that just drop. It was a well-intended idea, but it wasn't a good idea.

Not when I was going to be leaving for Portugal after the new year.

But then I hadn't planned on bringing Emma to Houston for what couldn't be called anything other than a date.

An unintended date, perhaps, but a date nonetheless.

I'd finally brought a girl to my favorite little French restaurant and it seemed fitting that the girl was Emma.

She'd been staring at the menu, though, for far too long.

"Are you okay?" I asked.

"I'm okay," she said with a tight little smile that told me something was bothering her.

It might have been ten years since I'd spent time with her, but I knew Emma.

As I sat here, looking at Emma over my open menu, I realized that she and I had been closer than I had been to any girl since.

We'd dated longer and we had been closer.

She glanced up at me from beneath those dark lashes, then realizing I was looking at her, she lowered her menu and met my gaze.

"What?" she asked.

"Nothing," I said with a little shake of my head. I looked down at my menu. I couldn't answer even her if I wanted to.

My throat was full and I was overwhelmed by the moment.

I shouldn't have brought her here. Being here with her like this brought back too many emotions. Emotions I didn't even realize I'd been harboring all these years.

I'd been the one to go off to college and leave her. I'd barely thought anything about it. At least not that I would admit. Even to myself.

Sure. I'd thought about her. A lot.

And no other woman had ever compared to her.

But I'd been so focused on learning to fly and flying. Airplanes. Helicopters. That I had barely thought about anything else. The myth about pilots having a one track mind was absolutely true.

But now that I had the flying down. Didn't mean I didn't still love it. And didn't mean that there were very few things I'd rather be doing. Didn't mean that I wouldn't rather be here with Emma than anywhere else.

Even more than in an airplane. Or even a helicopter.

Chapter Twenty-Four

Emma

Our server served us ice cold water from a carafe and brought us an appetizer of olives, cheese, and chilled boiled shrimp with spicy cocktail sauce.

An interesting combination.

There were people at three other tables. Three business men in suits at one table. Probably attorneys from across the street.

An older man and woman with papers on their table, obviously conducting some kind of business deal.

The third table had two younger men wearing ties. A business lunch, I decided.

The restaurant looked like the kind of place a man would bring a date, especially with the lady's menus with no prices. Maybe it was more of a dating venue at night.

It was the middle of the afternoon, so that could be a good explanation why there were only business people here.

I thought about asking Theodore, but right now I was feeling rather cross with him.

He could have asked me to come to his house for Christmas and I might would have done so. But instead, he'd admitted that it was Genevieve's idea.

I wouldn't go unless it had been his idea. The fact that it wasn't his idea told me a lot.

It confirmed that he'd brought me to lunch as a friend.

He'd held my hand as we walked on the roof and crossed the street.

Of course he had. He was a gentleman.

"Are you okay?" he asked.

"I'm okay." I nodded. Or maybe more accurately I would be okay.

I'd read too much into the last couple of days.

I blamed Doreen and Grandma. They had put fanciful ideas in my head about Theodore dating me. Doreen had even suggested he wanted to marry me.

Doreen didn't know. She and Grandma lived in another world. They lived in the past. A past where people still wanted to get married and live in a small town for the rest of their lives.

Not Theodore. There was no way Theodore would consider doing more than just stopping off in Maple Creek to see his family for the holidays.

Not that he was seeing much of them, but they were probably at work today, so he got a pass for that.

Last night? He got a pass for that, too. Just because.

But my life was in Maple Creek with Grandma. I was the one taking care of her.

As a result, Theodore and I would never have lives that matched up.

I shouldn't even be thinking about it.

I shook off the thought and forced myself to put things back into the perspective where they belonged.

It was a friendly lunch.

He and I had spent a lot of time together in our past. Although he had no way of knowing it, he knew me more than anyone else had ever known me.

It was logical that he would want to share his love of flying the helicopter with me. Of course he would.

And he'd brought me to an upscale restaurant because it was the kind of place he gravitated to as a pilot.

I just had to keep my head about me and make sure I didn't fall in love with him all over again.

There was only one problem with that.

I was already predisposed to being in love with him.

And not only that. I had never stopped.

Chapter Twenty-Five

THEODORE

By the time our entrees arrived, Emma seemed to have gotten past whatever it was that had been bothering her.

I couldn't even begin to think what I'd said that had troubled her.

We'd talked about her parents. Maybe that was it.

Maybe her parents couldn't afford to fly to Maple Creek for the holidays. Flights were expensive these days. They were retired, so they had the time, but that didn't mean that they had the money.

Maybe I would explore that with her a little more. Later.

It wasn't really my business.

But I might be in a position to help out. If that was the problem.

That was the only thing I could think of really that might be troubling her.

I'd invited her, in a roundabout way, to spend Christmas with me and my family. Maybe that had thrown her off guard.

I'd ask her again later.

"This is a really nice restaurant," she said.

"I think so, too. I don't mind a crowded restaurant, but sometimes I'm in the mood for a quieter place."

"Like today?"

I shrugged. "Maybe. I just thought you'd like it."

"You made a good choice," she said. "It must be more popular in the evenings."

"Maybe," I said. "Probably. I've never been here in the evenings."

She nodded and watched me over the rim of her water glass. I got the sense that she was analyzing everything I said.

Maybe it was because she was a psychologist.

I decided to ask her.

"Are you analyzing me?"

She bit back a laugh. "Why would you ask me that? I don't just go around analyzing people."

"Maybe you can't help it. It's what you do."

"Only when I'm working," she said with a little smile.

"So you can just turn it off when you're not working?"

"Maybe I turn it on when I am working. Sort of like how you turn on thinking about flying a helicopter.

"Maybe."

Even though she denied it, I had a feeling she might be minimizing just how much she used her psychological skills.

"I'd love to know what's going on in your head right now," I said, mostly just to toy with her.

"Oh no," she said, looking a little startled. "You wouldn't like it. I'm just a simple girl with simple thoughts."

"Somehow I doubt that. But you're right. I probably wouldn't like it. But not because you're simple. Because I'd probably be lost in a maze of complexity."

She made a sound that sounded something like a strangled laugh and stabbed a piece of lettuce.

"I think you're projecting," she said.

"Hardly. Genevieve told me just this morning that men are simple creatures and I tend to believe her."

"We will agree to disagree," she said. "You don't seem to be part of the gossip mill around Maple Creek. What have you been doing? Besides flying helicopters?"

"That's been exactly what I've been doing for the last few months."

"Grandma says I should ask you where you live."

I was pretty sure I managed to keep my expression blank. If I let my reaction show at all, Emma would have noticed. That was one of the problems with psychologists. They didn't miss anything.

"I've been living in Austin," I said. It wasn't a lie. It was in fact the truth. I had been living in Austin. I just wasn't going to be living in Austin anymore.

"Do you like it?" she asked.

"It's not Houston. But it's okay. I met a lot of good people." Influential people. People who had a lot of money and access to good career opportunities all over the world.

"Do you ever think about moving to Houston?"

I felt myself mentally taking a step back. After my conversation with Genevieve this morning, I was overly cautious about what I was going to tell Emma and not tell her.

I was not going to tell her that I had decided to move to Portugal. Not now. Not today.

Maybe I wouldn't even tell her at all.

Maybe I would just let history repeat itself.

"Maybe. I don't think I'll be staying in Austin."

"You have other plans?"

"I'm still trying to figure that out. My brother-in-law James want me to be part of a business venture here."

"Flying helicopters?"

"Yes."

"But doesn't he work for Noah Worthington at Skye Travels?"

"I'm not quite sure how, but Noah is involved in his deal."

"I would expect nothing less. If it flies, Noah Worthington has his hand in it."

"That is pretty much true." And it was one of the reasons I had to move to Portugal to pursue private flying that didn't involve Noah and Skye Travels.

At the moment, however, that was just something between me and myself.

"Tell me something about you."

Chapter Twenty-Six

Emma

The restaurant cleared out, all the business people going back to their offices, leaving just me and Theodore as the only customers.

No one seemed to mind. Our server, in fact, told us to take our time. To enjoy the quiet before the storm.

At least now I knew that the restaurant would be getting busy again with an evening crowd.

Theodore had been partially right. I might not actively analyze people on my time off, but I noticed certain things. It was impossible for me not to.

For example, I noticed that I must have touched on something Theodore didn't want to talk about. He didn't want to talk about his business plans.

That made me all the more curious.

"Are you considering the business venture with your brother-in-law?"

"I'm trying to figure how to be part of it in some way."

"But not the way he's asking."

Theodore looked at me sideways.

"That's correct, Dr. Flynn."

I just smiled.

"Have you thought about going to work for Noah?" I asked.

"You know. It's odd. All the men in my family work for Noah Worthington. I've never even met him."

"I hear he's a really good man."

"I'm sure he is, but I'm not a jump on the bandwagon kind of guy."

"No. I don't suppose you are," I said, considering. Hadn't I just been thinking that very thing about Theodore. More specifically that moss didn't grow under his feet.

The server stopped by our table and changed out our candle with a fresh one, carefully lighting the wick.

"Do you think we've overstayed our welcome?" I asked after he walked out of earshot.

"I don't know. Why would they care?"

"We're taking up space."

He glanced around at the empty tables.

"Good point," I said.

"I'll leave him a big tip. He'll be happy."

I decided to let Theodore off the hook for now. I had a feeling he wasn't telling me everything about what he was doing in his career.

But he wasn't my client or my student. It wasn't my job to get him to open up about whatever it was he was avoiding.

I decided to put my money where my mouth was and at least try to turn off my psychology skills.

"I hear you're going to be an uncle," I said.

"You heard right," he said, but he didn't look happy about it like I had expected him to.

Most people were excited about becoming an aunt or uncle. In fact, I'd yet to meet anyone who wasn't.

Until now.

"You don't seem happy about it."

"It quite frankly terrifies me."

Chapter Twenty-Seven

Theodore

Sitting in the shadowy ambiance of the French restaurant, drinking sparkling water—a pilot never drank alcohol when he was anywhere near flying—it was easy to talk to Emma.

Maybe it was too easy to talk to her.

She was a little too good at getting me to talk, despite what she said about not analyzing people when she wasn't working. She might not be analyzing me, but she was using her psychological wiles, not to be confused with feminine wiles.

"What terrifies you about becoming an uncle?" Emma asked. I could tell she was trying not to laugh about this very serious subject.

"I'm not sure," I said. "A lot of things."

"Want to share?"

"Seriously?"

"Yes. I admit I'm curious. I've never known anyone who was terrified about becoming an uncle."

"Not terrified like being afraid of clowns or anything like that," he said.

"Then terrified how?"

I could be honest with Emma. Just because I wasn't ready to tell her that our history was repeating itself, didn't mean I couldn't be honest with her about my feelings.

"I think it's one of those turning points in life where everything changes. Once one of my siblings brings another life into the world, there's no going back."

"There's no going back anyway," she said softly.

"I *know* that. But it's like a kind of signpost. I can almost hear the gates closing behind me."

"I can see how that would be terrifying."

"Then there's the pressure. What if I'm not a good uncle? What if I'm not around enough?"

And that, I realized was the heart of the matter. Moving to Portugal meant I would most definitely not be around, not only not enough, but not at all.

I would not be around at all.

"I'm sure you'll be fine. Everyone worries about how they'll deal with change."

"Right." There was no way she could understand. She couldn't understand because I hadn't told her.

Maybe I should just tell her now.

Then I could stop worrying about it.

Besides, it just felt wrong to get close to her again only to drop the bomb on her about leaving. I'd done that once. I did not want to do it again.

"You're phone is vibrating," Emma said.

"It's okay," I said, but I turned my phone over and looked at the name. "I actually need to take this. It's James."

"Go ahead," she said with a little wave of her hand.

"Excuse me." I stood up. "James." I paced across the room, the phone pressed against my ear.

James knew I was borrowing the helicopter.

Just as I knew that business superseded my date with Emma.

"Noah wants to meet with us at the airport," James said.

"Okay. When?"

"In an hour."

"An hour? I've got Emma with me."

"It's okay. He understands. He puts family first anyway."

I didn't bother to tell James that Emma wasn't technically family. Maybe there had been a time when she would have been. Almost was. But at the moment, she was a friend.

I had to keep her as a friend. I couldn't let her slide back into being more.

Not when I was going to leave her all over again.

Chapter Twenty-Eight

Emma

"Speak of the devil," Theodore said, coming back to the table.

"James?"

"Noah Worthington."

"That was Noah?"

"No. But Noah wants to meet with James and me in..." I glanced at my watch. "an hour. At the Houston Airport."

"Oh. Do you have time to get me home? And back? Of course not."

"It's okay," he said with a little smile. "Looks like we just get to make a little detour. Do you mind?"

"Of course not." I certainly didn't mind the distraction from my statistics textbook.

"I'll be right back."

Theodore tracked down the server and handed him a credit card. Seemed I wasn't going to even get a glimpse of the check.

Curious, I googled the restaurant.

"What are you doing?" Theodore asked, picking up my coat.

"Nothing," I said, putting my phone away.

He smiled. "Don't do it."

"I don't know what you're talking about," I said as I slipped my arms into my coat as he held it for me.

"You know exactly what. If you look it up, you'll lose the romance of it."

"Is that so?" It was interesting that he thought of the lady's menu as being romantic.

"Yes. That is so. If you look it up, I'll know."

"You will not."

We waved at our server as we walked toward the exit. James opened the door and cold air struck us in the face.

"When did it get so cold?" I asked.

"It's supposed to be cold. It's Christmas," he said.

"Now I know you grew up in the same town I did. And I know you know that it's rarely this cold on Christmas in Houston."

"Again," he said. "You have to let yourself believe in the magic."

Theodore was acting a little strange, even for him.

He took my hand as we walked quickly down the sidewalk back toward the building where we had parked.

With the clouds that had moved in, the metal Christmas trees lining the street twinkled with festiveness.

Cars passed, bumper to bumper on Post Oak Boulevard. Rush hour.

But we didn't have to be part of the rush hour traffic. We would just go up and fly right above it.

Into the building, up the elevator, and out onto the helipad.

Now this, I thought, as he helped me climb inside the helicopter was magical.

Flying in a helicopter with the man I'd been in love with since that day we'd met in the coffee shop.

"It's cloudy," I said, as the helicopter roared to life. "Can we still fly?"

"It's not bad," he said, looking at the radar on his iPad, then looking up at the sky through the window. "It's not bad at all."

He made some adjustments on the computers, then turned to look at me.

"Are you scared?"

"No," I said with a smile. "I'm not scared."

I wasn't scared. Not with Theodore.

He was the one person I'd always felt safe with. That hadn't changed.

Chapter Twenty-Nine

THEODORE

We landed on the new Skye Travels helipad at the airport.

The Skye Travels helipad.

Noah Worthington apparently was taking his time growing his helicopter business.

As a billionaire with a company worth billions, he wasn't doing it for the money. Even though I wasn't a billionaire, I understood the concept of wanting a new challenge.

I'd done the same thing on a smaller scale. I'd gone from being a successful, proficient airplane pilot—licensed to fly all sorts of different airplanes, the Cessna, The Phenom, the Lear—to learning how to fly helicopters.

I'd needed a challenge in my life and pursuing that challenge had opened all sorts of new doors for me.

It had gotten me job opportunities that hadn't been available to me as an airplane pilot. Having the skills to fly both types of aircraft, airplane and helicopters, was rather unusual for a pilot. Most pilots had a passion for one or the other.

I loved flying airplanes. But now I was loving flying helicopters. Unlike an airplane, I could land a helicopter just about anywhere, including on top of a building.

Couldn't do that with an airplane.

"Do you want me to wait here?" Emma asked, after we landed and I powered off the helicopter.

"What? Of course not. You have to come in with me."

"I don't mind." She pulled her coat tighter.

"I'm not leaving you out here to freeze. Come on."

I took off her headset and set it aside.

After I helped her out of the airplane, I took her hand as we walked across the tarmac.

I knew I was making a statement by holding her hand.

Noah's office windows looked out over the tarmac.

He would see us as would my brother-in-law. James's car was in the private parking area. He must have already been on his way to the airport when he'd called me.

Maybe I was staking my claim on Emma. Or maybe it just quite simply felt right to hold her hand.

I'd worry about that later.

We went inside the Skye Travels building, went up the elevator to the second floor where the offices were. I gave Emma's hand a squeeze and released it before we stepped off the elevator.

The less I had to explain when I left for Portugal, the better.

"Theodore?" The receptionist said. "Mr. Worthington is expecting you. You can go on back."

"I'll just wait out here," Emma said.

"Come with me," the receptionist told her. "We'll get you something to drink."

I hesitated. But the receptionist, Betty, according to the name plate on the desk, was already motioning Emma to follow her in the other direction.

With little else to do but to find my way down the hallway toward Noah's office, I did just that. Not knowing my way, although Betty seemed to think that I should, I followed the sound of James's voice.

I found him in a corner office sitting with a sophisticated, dignified older man with a full head of short neatly trimmed gray hair.

Noah stood up as James introduced us. He was a tall, imposing man, looking every bit the successful businessman he was.

"It's a pleasure to finally meet you," Noah said. "The last of the Devereaux brothers."

"It's an honor, Sir," I said. "Needless to say, I've heard a lot about you."

"Hopefully not all bad. Have a seat. We have some things to talk about."

As I sat in one of the three chairs with an unobstructed view of the tarmac, I glanced at James. What had he told Noah?

If the two of them put me on the spot, I might be forced to reveal my hand.

I might not be ready to tell people I was taking a position in

Portugal, but if push came to shove, they might leave me no choice but to come clean.

The more people I told, the more likely it was to get back to Emma.

I might be reluctant to tell my family or even Noah, but it seemed that I was finding it more and more impossible by the minute to tell Emma.

I'd put my chips in place and they were starting to fall.

Only now I wasn't so sure I liked the way I had set them up.

Portugal was a once in a lifetime opportunity. I just had to keep telling myself that.

It would all work out.

Chapter Thirty

Betty led me back to a private lounge area designated for board members.

"This room is for Skye Travels board members, Noah and his wife, and of course, meetings."

"It's lovely," I said, looking up at the glass roof just as a small airplane flew over.

There were floor to ceiling windows on one wall and a view overhead.

"The room was designed by Mr. Worthington's granddaughter. She's an architect."

"Impressive. It's new then."

"Quite new," she said. "I can still smell the paint."

"Maybe a little," I said. "Now that you mention it. It definitely smells clean."

"What would you like?" she asked. "A latte? A mimosa? A sparkling water?"

"Just water," I said.

"Alright." Betty pulled a bottle of water out of a clear cooler, opened the top, and poured sparkling water into what looked like a crystal glass.

"You're very kind," I said.

"Have a seat," Betty said as she poured a glass of water for herself.

We sat on a buttery soft leather sofa facing the windows.

Betty acted less like a receptionist and more like a hostess.

"How long have you and Theodore been together?" she asked.

I paused with my glass of water halfway to my lips.

I liked to think that I was astute when it came to situations like this.

Betty had brought me into the VIP room thinking that I was Theodore's girlfriend or maybe even more than a girlfriend. If she discovered that I was no more than just friend and was only by a quirk of chance, she might just toss me out of here on my ears.

I decided to ere on the side of caution.

"We started dating when we were freshmen in high school."

"Oh my. You've been together a long time."

"It was a long time ago," I said, evasively.

"Well, I hope that Theodore and James can work out an agreement with Mr. Worthington so that we get to see more of you."

"I'd like that," I said.

"What do you do, Dear?"

"I'm a psychology professor and I do some private practice on the side."

"Well. Isn't that something? Mrs. Worthington, Noah's wife, is a psychologist, too."

"I think someone mentioned that," I said. I had heard it somewhere, but I couldn't remember where. "She must have a lot of clients."

"She's actually very selective. She rarely takes on anyone new these days."

"I'm afraid I don't have the luxury of turning people away," I said.

"Oh, you will, Dear," she said. "What Mr. Worthington is proposing will make Theodore a very wealthy man."

"Oh." I suddenly felt like an intruder. Like Betty was telling me things she shouldn't because she thought I was with Theodore.

Surely she saw I wasn't wearing a ring.

She was jumping to a lot of assumptions.

I considered telling her... something. That Theodore and I had been together at one time, but we weren't together anymore?

A chime that I barely heard caught Betty's attention.

"I have to get to the front desk," she said. "Please. Make yourself at home. Sometimes these negotiations can go on for some time."

After she left, I sat staring out the window. A small jet with the Skye Travels logo splashed across the fuselage came in for a landing.

Theodore had seemed to think that this meeting would be brief and we would be on our way back to Maple Creek.

Betty, on the other hand, seemed to think that the meeting was not only very important, but would take a long time.

It was all very curious.

I had quite simply been at the right place at the right time.

Most of my experience was at the university level.

This billionaire dollar business world was new to me.

Unfortunately, I wasn't about to assume that even if Theodore worked out a business deal with Mr. Worthington that I would coming back.

As of right now, I was simply Theodore's ex-girlfriend.

I wouldn't mind it if there was more to our relationship, but I had been there and done that. Theodore was a rolling stone and a wise woman would be smart to not get too attached.

I wasn't sure whether I fit into the category of a wise woman or not, at least not where it came to Theodore.

When it came to Theodore, all bets were off.

Chapter Thirty-One

THEODORE

My meeting with James and Noah Worthington lasted just under ninety minutes.

I knew because I noted the time and about every couple of minutes I wondered what Emma was doing.

Fortunately I was good at multi-tasking that way.

Noah served us some sparkling non-alcoholic juice that tasted a lot like champagne to me.

A lot of pilots drank when the mood struck them, but not Skye Travels pilots.

Noah had a very strict bottle to throttle policy.

One drink could get a man grounded from flying. Two drinks could get him put on probation. And three drinks would have him in rehab.

I knew this already just from listening to my brothers.

I respected Noah for his strict policies.

Give a man an inch and he would take a mile. That's what I always said.

So we drank our sparkling juice as Noah and James discussed their business venture regarding a helicopter service in the Houston area.

Noah stood up and walked to the windows as one of his airplanes took off.

While there was a lull in the conversation, I spoke up.

"How do I fit into all this?" I asked.

"We need someone to run the business," Noah said without hesitation.

"Of course," I said. "But you have a big family, Mr. Worthington. You have a lot of pilots in your family who would more than qualify."

"You're right," he said, turning back around to face me. "But they're all airplane pilots."

I glanced at James.

"Surely you have someone who's good at business."

Noah quickly dismissed the idea.

"We need someone who knows how to fly helicopters. I'm learning, but I'm far from proficient. Besides, if I take on one more thing, I'll have to answer to my wife and that won't be pretty."

"I understand." I looked to my brother-in-law. "What about James?"

"No," James said quickly. "I'm about to start a family."

I stared at James a moment wondering, hoping he wasn't,

trying to tell me something about becoming an uncle. Surely not him, too.

"I see." I sat back, holding my glass of sparkling juice, then took a long drink.

This was one of those times when something stronger would be more than welcome.

I was having one of those moments that jarred a man out of his comfort zone.

Some people might call it an epiphany. I just called it a realization.

I was being asked to take on a massive undertaking because I was a single man with no family.

I didn't plan on always being a single man with no family and I didn't like the assumption that I was available for such an endeavor.

I especially didn't like the assumption that I didn't have the potential to became a family man.

I had been okay with that unstated assumption when I'd been offered the job in Portugal.

But now the assumption wasn't so veiled.

They had all but said they wanted someone who could devote their life to this endeavor.

Noah had started his company, Skye Travels, and he'd done it while he was married.

So why was it so important that a family man like James be removed from their equation?

I didn't like it. I didn't like it one bit.

"I need some air," I said, standing up and walking out.

Chapter Thirty-Two

EMMA

I was sitting on the buttery soft leather sofa intermittently answering my emails and watching airplanes land and takeoff on the tarmac just outside the window.

I could just see the edge of the helicopter sitting on the helipad. I hardly would have noticed it if I hadn't flown here on it. I'd never really paid much attention to helicopters. Usually when a helicopter was involved, there was some kind of emergency.

Such was the way of growing up in a small town. Who would have thought that helicopters were used for luxury travel?

At one point, Betty had poked her head in, saying she was tied up with something, but to let her know if I needed anything. I didn't.

I didn't mind being here. If I weren't here, I would be at home, outlining a statistics textbook chapter.

I felt like I was getting a peek at a world most people never saw.

I was about to look up the percentage of the population that flew on private airplanes when Theodore came through the door.

He looked upset. I could tell by the set of his jaw as well as the agitation radiating off him.

"Hey," I said. "What's wrong?"

He shook his head and sat down, staring out the window at the airplanes on the tarmac.

"They want me to run a new division of Skye Travels."

"This is part of James's deal?"

"James had just told me he needed a pilot. He hadn't said anything about running anything."

"It's something you would be good at." It was just a guess, really, but I harbored the assumption that Theodore would be good at anything he set his mind to.

"Probably," he said, standing up again and walking to the window. He leaned against the glass, putting his weight on one arm.

A sleek Skye Travels private jet came in for a landing and taxied over not far from us, the loud roar of the engine filling the room.

As the noise faded, Theodore went to the bar and poured himself a glass of water.

Bringing his glass with him, he came back and sat on the sofa next to me, still staring straight ahead.

"But... it's not something you want to do."

He glanced over a me, his troubled blue eyes meeting mine for just a brief moment before he looked away again.

"How can I help?" I asked.

He took a deep breath and slowly let it out.

"It's a generous offer," he said.

"But it's not what you want to do," I said again.

"I could do it," he said, draining his glass.

"But..."

He got up. Paced back to the window and turned around to face me.

"I was actually going to do it. But somewhere else."

"How is this different?"

"They made an assumption," he said. "It didn't sit right with me."

"What kind of assumption?" I got up and refilled his glass.

"Thanks."

I raised an eyebrow at him in question.

"They assumed that I was the right person for the job only because I'm single."

I sat down again.

"That's rather odd. What if you don't plan on staying single?"

"Exactly," he said, giving me grateful glance.

"But. Did they actually say that was why?"

"They didn't have to."

"Then how do you know?"

"Because that's the reason James didn't take it."

"That's it?"

"That's it."

"Well. I don't know James, but I do know that he isn't you.

Just because he didn't want to take the job with a family on board, doesn't mean you can't."

He looked at me, but didn't answer.

"Come on," he said. "Let's go home."

I followed him out of the meeting room, down the hall, past the empty receptionist area, to the elevator.

Maybe I was the only person who knew just how hard it was to pin Theodore down to one place.

What Noah and James were asking was outside of his comfort zone.

But what I didn't understand was the reason he was giving me.

He wasn't saying he didn't want the job. That he didn't want to be tied down.

He was kind of saying the opposite.

I didn't understand.

Chapter Thirty-Three

I'd never stormed out of a meeting like that before.

Everything in my upbringing, everything about me professionally, urged me to go back and apologize. To hear Noah out. To be respectful of the man's time.

It was certainly what I *should* do. Right now, though, I didn't want to go back in there.

I just needed to get away.

It wasn't Emma's fault.

Something had simply come over me.

We strode across the tarmac to the helipad in silence. The air seemed colder than it had a couple of hours ago.

Maybe it was because the sun was setting on an already dreary day.

After we got loaded into the helicopter, I saw that the temperature was actually dropping. It wasn't just my imagination.

"Your phone's ringing," Emma said.

I pulled my phone out of my pocket. Looked at the screen.

"It's James," I said, putting it back in my pocket.

"You're not going to answer it?"

"I'll see him back at home later."

"Maybe he needs a ride."

I gave her a look and sent him a quick text.

> Getting ready to head home. Need a ride?

JAMES

> No. I drove. We'll talk when I get home.

"He doesn't need a ride," I told Emma.

"Good." She settled back in her seat and put on her headset.

Now that we were back in the helicopter, my blood was settling down.

"Sorry about that," I said, speaking through the headset, as I prepared to take the helicopter into the air.

"You don't have to apologize," she said. "I'm just worried about you."

"I'm a little disconcerted. I'll be okay."

"Thank you for the helicopter ride."

"Anytime," I said.

"Be careful with that," she said. "I could get used to this kind of travel."

I laughed.

"Do your brothers take you flying?"

"I've been up a couple of times."

"They should take you up more often."

"Probably," she said. "It's not something I want to get used to."

And that, I thought, was too bad.

Emma deserved to travel in style.

We were up now, in the air, traveling through the clouds, heading north toward Maple Creek.

"Betty thinks we're together," Emma said out of the blue.

"Together, together?"

"I think so. I evaded the question. I was afraid she would toss me out of the special conference room if I told her differently."

"She wouldn't do that," I said.

It was interesting that Betty thought that for one and it was also interesting that Emma hadn't corrected her.

I had a decision to make. I could wait until after Christmas, as Genevieve suggested, to tell Emma that I was moving to Portugal.

Or I could go ahead and tell Emma now.

Or maybe I would just not tell her at all.

Not telling her at all would be the coward's way.

I wasn't a coward. It wasn't my way.

Waiting until after Christmas seemed wrong, too. It felt like being deceptive through the holidays.

That wasn't right either.

My sister was wrong about that. Just because she didn't want to know until after Christmas, I couldn't keep something like that to myself.

I had to tell them. I had to tell Emma.

But I would wait, I decided, until we were back at her house.

Just in case she never wanted to see me again.

Chapter Thirty-Four

Emma

Theodore was acting strange.

I'd never known him to be so quiet and introspective.

I didn't mind, though. We made the relatively short flight in what felt like companionable silence.

Before landing at the airport in Maple Creek, he took me on a little scenic tour of the town.

Downtown was all lit up with its multi-colored Christmas lights. People walking here and there along the sidewalks as the number of shopping days until Christmas got fewer and fewer.

Houses were decorated for the holidays, some more than others.

After he took us down for a landing at the airport, we transferred from the helicopter to his car.

Although he opened the car door for me, held it open as I got in, and closed it behind me, I could tell that something was different with him.

I tried not to be paranoid. I tried not to think that it was directed at me.

It was virtually impossible, though.

He might not be upset with me, but I was the one he directed it toward. It might as well be me that he was upset was. The result was the same.

We drove without talking. I couldn't remember ever riding in a car with him, even back in high school, when we didn't talk about one thing or another, no matter how trivial. Sometimes we would just talk about the song on the radio, but it was always something.

This evening as the sun began to set, Theodore didn't even have the radio on. The only sound other than the normal road noises was the steady hum of the heater blowing warm air out of the vents.

It was almost as though he couldn't wait to get me home and out of the car.

Or so it seemed.

After pulling into the driveway, he put the car in park.

"I need to talk to you about something," he said. "before you go in."

Something slammed in my chest. It was dread, plain and simple.

"Can we go inside first?" I asked. "I need to check on my grandmother. I didn't plan on being out this late."

"Of course," he said. "I'll come around. Get your door."

I forced myself to breathe as he got out and came around the car.

I really did need to check on my grandmother. But also I wanted to put off what sounded like a serious conversation.

I knew how Theodore was. I knew he was only in Maple Creek temporarily.

Even a job offer that would keep him here had him acting disconcerted, maybe even angry.

Even knowing that, I didn't want to hear him tell me what I already knew.

I didn't want to hear him tell me that he wasn't going to take the job here. That he was going to take the other job, wherever it was.

Wherever it was he hadn't even told me. I just knew that it wasn't here.

He opened the door and held out a hand to assist me out.

I pulled my hand away under the pretense of looking for my key.

I had let myself have the day to pretend that we were back together. I'd even let Betty believe it and in letting Betty believe it, I'd all but believed it myself.

But now it was time to get back to reality.

Theodore would be moving on and I would be staying behind.

Just like last time.

It was happening all over again.

I had to guard my heart.

I could do that because this time I knew what to expect.

Chapter Thirty-Five

Theodore

By the time we got inside, Emma's grandmother was already in bed, reading.

Emma went around the house, checking the stove, the doors in what looked like rote behavior. Put a glass in the dishwasher. She did it all as though it was a habit she'd done a hundred times.

Then we sat on the sofa in her living room.

Someone had cleaned out the hearth where I'd had a fire going last night.

I imagined that someone was Emma.

It seemed that she was the one who took care of pretty much everything.

"Do you want me to bring in some firewood?" I asked.

"No," she said. "We don't have anymore."

"Oh." So I had used up the last of her firewood last night. It would have been nice to know that. I could have replaced it.

"What did you want to tell me?" she asked, sitting up straight, her hands clasped in her lap, taking a deep breath and looking at me with a blank expression.

She looked guarded. I hated being the one to put that expression on her face.

I would just about rather have a root canal right now than tell her what I had to tell her. But it had to be done. I had no choice. The longer I waited, the worse it would be.

"I'm not taking the job here," I said.

"I didn't think you would."

"I'm that predictable, huh?"

"I'm afraid so," she said with a tight little smile. "So you're taking the other job."

"I think it's the best offer."

"I see."

"Emma," he said, putting his hands on my shoulders and looking into my eyes.

I forgot to breath. This was just like that night he'd told me he was going to Auburn.

We'd had no discussion about it. He had quite simply decided on his own.

We were right back there again.

In fact, the déjà vu was so strong, I felt a little bit dizzy.

I closed my eyes.

"Emma. The other job is in Portugal."

I had sisters. I knew the look on Emma's face.

"I think I misunderstood you," she said, looking into my eyes.

"No," I said softly. "You didn't misunderstand."

She swayed a bit. Using my hands on her shoulders, I steadied her.

"But..." She focused her eyes on mine.

Good. She wasn't going to faint.

"Why? Why Portugal?"

"It's a very lucrative offer."

"Oh." She looked down. "I didn't realize you were driven by lucrativity."

"Is that a word?" I asked, feeling an odd sense of relief that I couldn't explain. "I thought everyone was."

"Not everyone." Looking up again, she searched my eyes. "I thought you were driven by flying."

A car with a loud muffler drove past on the street. A dog barked somewhere.

Everything seemed normal for a Maple Creek evening.

"I am," I said. "But..."

But I was twisted up.

Chapter Thirty-Six

EMMA

Portugal.

Theodore was moving to Portugal.

"This is worse than I thought," I said, mostly to myself.

"Worse than you thought?"

"I knew you would be leaving," I said. "I just didn't think." I ran a hand through my hair. "I just didn't think you'd be going to another country."

"I know," he said, looking away.

"Why?" I asked.

Letting me go, he sat back against the sofa and ran his hands along his thighs.

There was only one reason I could think of why a man would leave his family and move away to a foreign country. Especially when he had pretty much the same job offer right here where his family lived.

"You have a girlfriend there?"

"A girl—? No." He looked confused. "I don't have a girlfriend there. I don't have a girlfriend anywhere."

"Oh. Then. I don't understand."

"It's a once in a lifetime opportunity," he said.

"How so?"

"I'll be part of owner of the company right up front. A start-up investor."

There was more he wasn't telling me. There had to be more.

Surely there was more.

But I'd known he would be moving along. No moss growing under his feet. And this was the path he'd chosen.

I nodded, swallowing the pain that I knew would be there. It wasn't as bad as I had expected. Maybe because I'd known it was coming.

I stood up and held my chin high.

"I wish you well," I said, holding out a hand.

He took my hand, but made something that sounded like a growling sound, and pulled me into a hug.

I fit right into his arms. Just the way I always had. He held me close, giving me one of those hugs he was so darned good at. The kind that made me feel safe, protected, and... loved.

After a moment of hesitation, I rested my cheek against his chest as he rested his chin on the top of my head.

Wrapping my arms around his waist, I sighed, feeling the tension drain away.

It didn't matter that I knew he was going away.

He was here right now.

He held me close and I held him close right back.

This was a moment in time. Just one moment in time.

One of those moments that was free of the boundaries of time.

There was no past and there was no future.

There was quite simply just right now.

The seconds passed and turned into an indeterminate number of minutes.

It was on the tip of my tongue to ask him to stay.

Don't go.

But I knew Theodore. I knew that he was not one to stay put in one place for very long.

Going to Portugal was one of those pulls of adventure that he would be unable to resist.

It made him who he was.

I couldn't change him.

Even if I asked him to stay and he did, he wouldn't stay for long.

It wasn't in his nature.

It was best if I quite simply just let him go.

If you love someone let them go.

Or something like that.

I wasn't sure that old saying exactly applied in this case, but I told myself it did.

I held onto those words.

Those words allowed me to admit that I did indeed love him. Always had. Always would.

And because I loved him, it was okay to let him go.

I'm not sure which one of us pulled back first. I think we sort of pulled back together at the same time.

"Emma," he said.

"It's okay," I said. "I understand. I'll see you around."

I forced what I hoped came across as a smile onto my lips and turned to walk to the door.

He followed as I'd known he would.

I put a hand on the doorknob, but instead of opening it, I stopped and looked back at him.

"Thank you for telling me," I said. "I know it couldn't have been easy."

"I—"

"Goodbye Theodore." I opened the door and stepped aside for him to walk through. "Be safe over there."

"You too." He nodded once, then walked through the door.

I closed the door behind him—such a finalizing sound—locked it, then turned around to lean against the closed door.

I stood there until I heard his car door open. The motor started. He backed out of the driveway onto the street, leaving behind only an echo of his presence.

He was gone.

So this was it.

My knees too weak to hold me up any longer, I slid to the floor.

Chapter Thirty-Seven

THEODORE

The next morning I woke early.

I'd only slept about a total of maybe three hours anyway, so I just went ahead and got up.

The house was quiet at four in the morning. We had a lot of early risers in the family, but four a.m. was a little early for even the earlier of the early risers on a typical day.

I made a cup of hot coffee, as though I needed something else to keep me awake, but it was habit.

Holding the hot latte, I paced the kitchen.

Everything was clean and in its place. All decorated for Christmas. Dishcloths with little green Christmas trees and red ornaments embroidered on them.

Even my coffee mug was festive red with a green handle.

I stopped in front of the calendar at the family computer desk.

It was where my parents kept all their bills and invoices. The computer they used for budgeting and accounting.

There was a monthly calendar hanging on the wall. One of those with a different picture every month. This month was a bucolic scene of a sleigh holding two people all bundled up in warm red coats. An image depicting days gone by.

The twenty-fifth was marked with a big red circle.

Five days.

Five days until Christmas.

My family would carry on their traditions.

They would go shopping on Main Street. Make cookies and pies. Play board games and card games.

I was the only one in my family who was single.

A sixth wheel?

If I hadn't run into Emma, I would have been content to be that odd man out. To spend Christmas with my family.

But now that I had spent time with Emma... now that I had reawakened all those old feelings that I'd though were buried deep... I didn't think I could bear it.

I would be thinking about Emma the whole time.

Even more, I would be tempted to go see her.

But it wouldn't be fair to her. It wouldn't be fair to string her along when I knew I was leaving.

Unfortunately the Devereaux trait of making a decision and sticking to it, that trait that typically was what made us successful, was not necessarily always one of the easiest traits to carry.

I sat down at the breakfast table and pulled up the email that contained the job offer in Portugal.

I had negotiated a start date in January, but their preference had been that I go ahead and move over there. Get settled in.

It would be smoother if I went ahead and did just that. I needed to go ahead and get there. Find a place to live, preferably a furnished place since I wasn't bringing any belongings other than some clothes and personal items with me.

I'd never bought a lot of furniture and I'd certainly never bought a house.

It made moving around easier.

Being almost thirty-years-old, it was probably about time for me to think about getting a place of my own. Maybe buying some quality furniture and settling in.

Moving to a new country was taking my freedom to move around to a whole new level.

Today, I decided. Today I would tell my family. Then tomorrow I would get on a commercial flight and get myself to Portugal.

It was time to stop talking about it and do it.

My family would be okay. They wouldn't even miss me.

They had their lives.

It was time I started one of my own.

Chapter Thirty-Eight

Emma

Three Days Before Christmas

I'd taken the day off from lecture preparation to accompany my grandmother and Doreen downtown to do some last minute Christmas shopping.

It was one of those cold, dreary days that would have been better with snowfall.

As it was, it was just cold and dreary.

Maybe I should think about moving north where it actually snowed.

Maybe one day.

It wasn't likely that I was going to be able to talk my grandmother into moving. She was a Maple Creek girl through and through.

And it was just as doubtful that I could talk Zoe into moving in with her or letting Grandma move in with Zoe. Zoe was something of a free spirit who didn't want responsibility beyond her work at the bakery. Laser focused, she wanted to open her own bakery one day. In Maple Creek.

Grandma seemed to be doing better lately, but then it could be because I was, for the most part, keeping her out of the kitchen.

I did all the cooking and cleaning. Sometimes when I went to the Piggly Wiggly, I took Grandma with me. Grandma and Doreen usually.

No. I was pretty much stuck where I was.

My companions were a couple of old ladies.

They weren't bad as far as companions went. Grandma had been spending a good bit of time over at Doreen's house. Doreen was about the same age as Grandma, but she didn't seem to have any memory problems.

Her two grown children were coming in today or maybe it was tomorrow, so Doreen was excited about getting everything ready for them and Grandma was helping her.

As for me, I'd found it better not to think.

As long as I didn't think too much, I could go about my day feeling numb enough that thinking wasn't required. Yes. It was a vicious cycle that I purposely perpetuated.

I sat on one of the benches outside Hometown Threads, put the shiny red reflective bag I was holding for Doreen on the seat beside me, and idly watched the pattern of twinkling Christmas lights outlining the door of the store.

Sending my parents a gift card to Florida had been easy. They didn't expect anything to begin with, so a gift card was easier than shipping a gift.

I'd gone against everything I believed in and given in and bought gift cards for Zoe and Grandma. I'd even bought one for Doreen.

Zoe had asked me about driving back into Houston for another day of shopping, but I'd made excuses.

I didn't have the heart or the energy to do much more than get through my days.

I assumed Theodore was still in Maple Creek with his family, but I really didn't want to know one way or the other.

It was best if I didn't think about Theodore at all.

All the old feelings that I was supposed to have tamped down into the inaccessible areas of my memory were right there all over again. Right at the surface.

It didn't help that every corner of Maple Creek reminded me of him in one way or another.

I'd stepped out when I heard someone talking about Theodore.

"He moved to Portugal," someone said.

They kept talking as I stepped out the front door of the shop, but I tuned it out, refusing to listen. I'd heard enough. So he had already moved away. Either that or the gossipers had gotten it wrong. Either way I didn't want to know.

Homestead Threads reminded me of the dress I'd bought for our lunch date that wasn't supposed to have been a date, but had turned out to be a date after all. One of the best dates I'd ever had. With anyone. Ever.

The coffeeshop on the corner where we had met the first time and then where we had met the second time, too. What were the odds? It was almost like time had circled back around and put us right back where we had started.

Or so I had almost let myself believe. Almost.

A small jet flew past overhead. Probably one of the Devereaux boys.

It was low enough I caught sight of the Skye Travels logo splashed across the fuselage. It circled around and went around going in for a landing.

I'd always thought that flying via private jet would be the way to go. And I still believed it would be the best way to travel for long distances.

But for short distances, like from Maple Creek to Houston or even just across the city itself, a helicopter would be the way to go. A helicopter could land places an airplane couldn't even begin to think about landing. With ease.

Someday, I mused, airplanes would be replaced by some futuristic version of helicopters.

They had to be.

Helicopters were just so darn cool.

Grandma and Doreen came out, bearing shopping bags, all happy smiles with their newfound treasures.

I got up and took the bags from them.

It was silly, but their happiness made me feel even worse.

It was Christmastime and my heart was broken all over again.

Even if Theodore walked down the street right now, I might be civil, but I wasn't sure I could give him another chance.

He'd broken my heart twice. Surely that was enough.

Fortunately, perhaps, it wasn't something I would have to find out.

In all fairness, it hadn't been his fault this time. I'd sort of broken my own heart by daring to imagine that there was something there with nothing to indicate that there was.

I could hardly put that on Theodore.

"Ooh. Let's get ice cream," Grandma said as we passed the ice cream shop.

"It's too cold for ice cream," Doreen said, hugging her heavy coat close.

"Ice cream is best when it's cold," Grandma said. "Right Emma?"

"Right," I said, absently, forcing myself to smile.

It seemed like I was forcing myself to smile a lot these days.

With Theodore moving to Portugal, it was all I could muster.

Before I found out he was moving away, I'd taken comfort in just knowing he was out there. Portugal was still out there, of course. It just wasn't out there in my world. Portugal was another world away. Not somewhere I would ever go and not somewhere Theodore could visit from easily. Not even as a pilot.

The funny thing about it was I didn't even realize it until now how much comfort I took from him being somewhere nearby. The things we took for granted without even realizing it.

Chapter Thirty-Nine

THEODORE

I made it all the way to New York before the winter storm hit.

It was a whiteout situation that shut down the entire city including the airport.

It was three days before Christmas and I was stuck in an airport in New York.

I sat in a plastic chair with my carryon bag at my feet. I'd had lunch in the private lounge and when I'd stepped out, everything was chaos.

When I checked with the scheduling desk, the young lady with long blonde hair pulled up into a high swinging ponytail was no help.

"I'm sorry, Sir. We have to wait until after the storm before we can start rescheduling flights."

"So the airport is closed. Officially."

"That's right," she said, with a bit of an attitude.

"Thanks for your help," I said, ignoring that attitude. I actually had a good reason for asking.

I needed to know if any plane could get in or out.

After plugging my cell phone into the charging tree, I stood up to stretch my back.

A family sat across from me. A mother, father, and four children. A family of six.

I came from a family of seven, but it was close enough to leave me feeling a bit homesick.

Our family had never gone on a family vacation, not all together. We'd been so far apart in ages that it had just never been something we'd done.

We'd gone places, instead, in small groups. Our parents made sure to spend time with all of us.

Everyone traveled so much for work that traveling for pleasure didn't enter into the equation. Staying home together was something we all enjoyed instead.

A tall, lanky teenager wearing a sweatshirt came up and plugged in his phone next to mine. He appeared to be travelling alone. Probably traveling home for Christmas or maybe going to visit extended family. He looked a little young to be a college student, but it was hard for me to tell anymore. Being almost thirty, it was getting harder and harder for me to tell an older high school student from one of the younger college students.

He could be coming home from boarding school, as I had done, but his hair was too long and he wasn't dressed like he'd come from boarding school. I would know. I'd made that trip home from boarding school often enough.

I wondered what it would have been like to travel as a family.

I liked to think that if I had a wife and children of my own, we would travel places. Maybe the Grand Canyon. Or Mackinac Island. Or...

And there it was.

Right there in the middle of my musings.

When I pictured myself traveling with a family of my own, I automatically pictured myself traveling with Emma.

Had Emma always been my prototypical wife?

Maybe she had and I hadn't even realized it.

It would explain a lot. It would explain why I had never seen any of the women I had dated as potential wives.

I could count on one hand the number of serious relationships I'd had since I'd left Maple Creek and Emma.

In my mind, Maple Creek and Emma were pretty much synonymous. It was hard for me to think of one without the other.

Sure. I'd been home for Christmas every year and somehow I'd never run into her. My family mostly stayed out at our house, though, only going into town and walking down Main Street on Christmas Eve to do some last minute shopping, having ice cream, and just enjoying being out together.

It was probably the closest we ever got to all of us going somewhere together.

Emma and her family, like most families, were probably at home on Christmas Eve watching a movie or playing games or whatever they happened to do on Christmas Eve.

In high school, Emma had gone with us on Christmas Eve. It had never really been quite the same for me after we broke up.

I couldn't walk down Main Street in Maple Creek without looking for, hoping to catch a glimpse of her.

And then this year, there she was. In the very same coffee shop where we had first met.

And now not only could I not think about having a family without thinking about her or even think about being with my own family at Christmas without thinking about her, but I couldn't sit in a New York Airport without thinking about her.

What made me think that if I went to Portugal, I wouldn't think about her there, too?

As far as I could figure, absolutely nothing.

Pulling my iPad out of my carryon bag, I checked the radar.

The snowstorm was going to be out of here by morning.

It would take the airport a little while to get up and running, flights rescheduled, and all that, but there were other ways to travel besides by airplane.

I unplugged my phone and dialed James's number.

"Hey buddy," I said. "I hate to ask, but I think I need your help."

Chapter Forty

EMMA

Christmas Eve had always been my favorite time of year.

Part of that came from fond memories of walking down Main Street with the Devereaux family on Christmas Eve. It was one of their traditions and I was always invited.

We'd meander through the shops, not so much for shopping, though sometimes we'd find a perfect last-minute gift, but to be part of the Christmas Eve magic.

My own family never did anything especially special on Christmas Eve. Our traditions were more on Christmas Day.

I'm sitting next to Zoe at the island in my grandmother's house following my sister's directions on making what she called her magical sugar cookies. Apparently it was a recipe she had created herself and had nothing to do with the bakery.

"When are you going to open your own bakery?" I asked her. She made measuring and stirring look like child's play while I painstakingly measured everything exactly and still my dough didn't look as smooth as hers did.

We already had two dozen cookies cooling on racks waiting to be frosted.

Grandma was sitting at the breakfast table adding red food coloring to homemade icing Zoe had "whipped up."

"And what are we going to do with all these cookies?" I added as an afterthought.

Zoe paused stirring with her wooden spoon and glanced at me.

"Probably never and I don't know yet."

"I thought opening your own bakery was your ultimate dream."

"Well," she said, stirring again. "My boss is thinking about retiring and letting me buy her out."

I bobbled my glass measuring cup and a little dust cloud of flour went all over my dark gray sweatshirt.

"Really? You're just now telling me this?"

"I just found out. And I wanted to think about it before I told you."

"Why?" I asked, cleaning spilled flour off the counter.

"I needed to think about it first."

"I see."

Since when had Zoe started thinking about things without telling me first?

Already independent, she was getting even more independent.

I hadn't even known that level of independence was possible in the little town of Maple Creek.

Apparently I'd had my head in the sand, especially when it came to my sister.

"That's great, Zoe," I said. "And what are we going to do with these cookies?"

Zoe and Grandma exchanged a glance.

I shrugged. It didn't really matter to me what we did with them.

I'd found that not caring so much about things freed up my mind to think about other things.

I was thinking about opening up a little office in town where I could see face to face clients. Grandma and Doreen were spending enough time together that I didn't have to be here all the time.

Besides, it gave me something to think about besides Theodore.

"First of all," Zoe said. "We're going to take some over to Doreen's house. Then we're going to take some to the police station downtown."

I glanced down at my flour coated sweatshirt with a instinctive sense of panic.

"When exactly are we planning on doing this?" I asked.

"As soon as we get these cookies baked and decorated," Zoe said, looking at me as though I'd asked which direction the sun rose in the mornings.

"I can't go like this," I said.

"I told you to wear an apron," Zoe said under her breath.

"Go ahead," Grandma told me. "Go get cleaned up. We'll finish up these cookies."

"Are you sure?" I asked.

Zoe glanced at Grandma.

"I'm sure," Zoe said. "We've got this."

As I left the kitchen, I heard them talking.

"At least she's starting to act like she cares," Grandma said.

"True. I was starting to worry."

Well. I started back toward my room to take a shower.

They didn't have to worry about me. I was going to be just fine.

And just because I could, I'd wear my new red sweater dress.

I didn't want anyone feeling sorry for me.

Chapter Forty-One

EMMA

Dropping the cookies off at Doreen's took a whole lot longer than any of us expected. Doreen was excited to introduce us to her two children and show off the tree they had decorated. Actually redecorated because Grandma and Doreen had done a good job of it weeks ago.

"Why don't the two of you go ahead to the police station?" Grandma asked. "I'm feeling a little tired."

"I'll make us some eggnog." Doreen offered. "Let Zoe and Emma go ahead."

So it was that Zoe and I took off down Main Street.

I felt a little like I had been tricked. Of course, I knew I was being paranoid. Zoe always took cookies to the police station on Christmas Eve. It was just that she had always taken them straight from work. Tonight she'd decided to go off on her own with her own private recipe.

With her boss retiring, it made sense that Zoe would start doing more and more things on her own.

But still I hadn't been walking down Main Street in Maple Creek on Christmas Eve since my senior year. Before Theodore had taken off.

Houston pretty much shut down on Christmas Eve. But not Maple Creek. Maple Creek was teeming with life. Families mostly and little groups of young people that escaped their families and came downtown for ice cream or just to walk around and hang out.

Everyone was bundled in their heaviest coats. Coats they would rarely have a use for.

Apparently even the bitter cold couldn't keep people from their traditional shopping experience downtown on Christmas Eve.

I looked up at the sky and wondered if there was snow in the forecast. I hadn't even checked. Another reminder of just how numb I was to everything Christmas right now.

As we made our way down Main Street, Christmas music spilled from external speakers. Colorful twinkling lights surrounding every door and every window. Draped over the little wooden boxes of ivies that had been there forever, I felt a lump in my throat.

I hadn't intentionally avoided downtown on Christmas Eve over the years, but maybe I had.

I remembered the magic, but tonight, it was as though everything was dull. Like being an extra in a black and white movie.

Without Theodore Devereaux, my Christmas Eve in Maple Creek had no color.

Shaking it off, I ran a hand down my red sweater dress. I'd lightly curled my hair, put on some makeup, and I knew I looked more like I belonged in Houston than Maple Creek.

I'd dressed up on purpose. To remind myself that I wasn't bound to Maple Creek. I was here by choice, but I didn't have to be.

I leaned close to Zoe to see what she was saying, but before I could figure it out, I looked up.

The Devereauxs were walking in our direction. I immediately recognized Genevieve and Anastasia walking in front, Christopher tailing behind them. The others were older and I didn't know them so well, but together they looked quite distinctive. Like they didn't belong in Maple Creek either and yet they were such a huge part of it.

I instinctively slowed my steps as did Zoe, but I involuntarily scanned the little group for Theodore. It didn't matter that I was pretty sure he had already left for Portugal. It was a reflex I couldn't control even if I wanted to.

I told myself I felt relieved that I didn't see him, but the truth was disappointment washed through me like a cold winter wind.

I hoped to just slip past them, unnoticed. I was so tired of forcing a smile on my face and it was going to be especially hard to do with Theodore's family.

But it wasn't meant to be.

Genevieve stopped right in front of me.

"Emma," she said, brightly, though I detected a little bit of surprise. "Hi. How are you?"

"Okay," I said. "We're just taking some cookies to the police department." I don't know why I felt compelled to explain to her why I was out on Christmas Eve.

Genevieve smiled at Zoe. "That's very nice of you." She obviously knew that Zoe was the baker in the family.

"Where's James?" I asked. Genevieve was newly married and it was a little odd to see her without him.

Genevieve smiled a little curiously. "He had... an errand to run."

"Oh. Right." It was Christmas after all. James was probably out getting her a last minute gift. Or getting firewood. Or there were any number of explanations for what kind of errand he could be running.

"Well," I said, ready to be on my way. "It was good to see you."

"It was good to see you, too."

The rest of Genevieve's family had walked on, leaving her behind.

"Do you have few minutes? To catch up?" she asked after a quick glance at Zoe then back to me. "Do you want to get some ice cream?"

I almost said it was too cold for ice cream. I didn't believe it, but I'd heard Doreen use it as an excuse, but Zoe answered before I could form an answer.

"That's a great idea," Zoe said. "I'll just run down to the police station and drop these cookies off."

"I don't want to put it off on you," I said.

Zoe lifted the tray she was carrying as though to illustrate that she was the one carrying the tray after all.

"Go," Zoe said. "Don't leave Genevieve alone."

I seriously doubted Genevieve would be alone. Her family was only a few yards away, but it seemed rude to not go.

And as uncomfortable as I was being around Theodore's family, I was even more uncomfortable being rude.

"I'll see you at home," Zoe said and she took off.

I followed Genevieve down the street.

"I just need to send a really quick text message," she said, pulling out her phone.

"Sure," I said. "Go ahead."

We stepped into the ice cream shop that smelled like vanilla, salted caramel, and freshly baked waffle cones. A little cinnamon and peppermint, too.

We sat on old-fashioned red stools at the little white bar and waited for our turn to order.

Happy Christmas music filled the room along with muted conversations from other customers. It was surprising just how many people were out getting ice cream on Christmas Eve. Taking a break from browsing through the stores.

A Christmas tree stood in one corner, decorated with little ice cream cone ornaments in all colors. The twinkling lights, ribbons, and bow at the top were in a pale blue that brought to mind the chilliness of winter and an elusively snowy Christmas Day.

Had it ever snowed in Maple Creek on Christmas Eve? Not that I could remember. If it had, it was before my time.

If it did snow, it would be nothing less than a miracle.

Miracles sometimes happened on Christmas, but not this Christmas.

This Christmas wasn't the one.

Chapter Forty-Two

Emma

As I sat with Genevieve on little red stools in the ice cream shop, I considered that she and I could have been friends and probably would have been if her brother and I had stayed together.

She had a way of making even an awkward situation not seem awkward.

We were both slowly eating our single scoops of chocolate vanilla swirl ice cream with caramel syrup drizzled over the top. Simple but decadent at the same time.

"I heard you'd been living in Houston before you came back to take care of your grandmother," she said.

"You heard right. Grandma is doing much better."

"Then your being here has been a good thing."

"I guess so."

"Right now I'm really enjoying living in Houston," she said. "James and I are taking advantage of everything. Plays. Concerts. Baseball games."

I was trying to figure out how to tell her that she was lucky. That when I lived in Houston, I rarely had time to do anything like that. I would have done it more if I'd had a boyfriend or a husband or even a best friend like her.

The door opened and she looked past me, her face brightening.

"There's James now," she said.

I turned around to say hello to James. He was looking quite handsome wearing his pilot's uniform.

"Hey Emma," he said after kissing his wife on the lips and taking her hand.

"Hi James."

My gaze flicked over his shoulder and I forgot to breathe.

I was certainly glad I was sitting down.

I blinked, thinking I was imagining things. The Devereaux boys all had a similar look.

But I knew Theodore. I knew him like I knew the back of my hand.

Even with the two-day scruff on his face, I knew him.

The curve of his lips. And his bluest of blue eyes. Eyes, that I noticed had little lines in the creases on either side.

I hadn't noticed those lines before.

He was tired.

I heard Genevieve and James saying something to each other, but I couldn't understand them. It sounded like they were somewhere off in the distance.

Theodore was the only person that existed for me right now.

"You're still here," I said, my voice sounding faint to my own ears.

"Thanks to James," he said with a glance at his brother-in-law. James and Genevieve had moved to a nearby table, leaving us alone.

"How so?"

"Let's just say I had a very long helicopter ride."

"From... Portugal?" I asked, knowing full well that civilian helicopters couldn't fly overseas.

He smiled and some of that tiredness left his eyes. He slid onto the stool next to mine, the one that Genevieve had just vacated.

"Something like that."

"I heard you had left already."

"You heard right."

"But..."

He glanced toward the window. "We made it just in time."

"What—?"

He slid off the stool. "Come with me," he took my hand, giving me no choice but to go with him.

He pushed open the door and we stepped outside into the bitter cold. A gust of wind whipped at my hair.

"What?" I asked, shoving my hair out of my eyes.

It was twilight now and the twinkling Christmas lights were in full color.

People were walking and laughing and looking up towards the sky.

Then I saw it.

Snow drifted down in big fluffy flakes, a flake landing on my eyelashes.

"Snow?" I looked up at Theodore.

"It's a Christmas miracle," he said. "Either that or I brought it with me from New York."

It struck me then what he had been trying to tell me.

He had just flown back from New York. In a helicopter.

So that was James's errand. Picking up Theodore.

"I've heard of that happening," I said, keeping a straight face.

In truth, it was all I could do to keep from grinning like a loon.

By whatever miracle or chance or whatever it was, Theodore was here. Standing with me in the falling snow. On Christmas Eve. Holding my hand.

"Why? Why are you here?" I searched his bluest of blue eyes for some kind of answer. For some kind of explanation.

"Because, my love," he said, softly as he gently swept a strand of hair off my cheek. "It occurred to me as I sat stranded in an airport in New York. Snowed in. That home is wherever you are."

Then with the snow falling around us like we were in our very own little magical snow globe, he kissed me.

Keep Reading for a Preview of
Her Christmas Rescue...

AUTHOR OF THE PRINCESS AND THE PLAYBOY

KATHRYN KALEIGH

Her Christmas
Rescue

A CHRISTMAS NOVEL

Chapter 1

TABITHA BLACK STOOD up and stretched, then tugged the sleeves of her sweatshirt down over her hands to combat the growing chill in the old building. She was exhausted, but the result was twofold. She was pulling her weight, and she was keeping her mind busy. She looked around at the open crates of merchandise, the contents of each box carefully inventoried and marked with prices. She sighed with a sense of accomplishment, even though she knew there was a long way to go. Putting the merchandise on the shelves was going to be an equally tedious project.

She walked to the front part of the store where her Aunt Allie was draping dark gray velvet ribbon on the Christmas tree. She was surrounded by glass and silver ornaments, from glittery balls to pewter magnolia flowers. Aunt Allie looked up and grinned at her. "Are you still at it?" she asked. "I thought you went on up to bed."

"No, but I've almost finished the inventory."

"Well, for goodness sakes," Aunt Allie said as she glanced at her watch. "I closed up two hours ago, and here we are still working."

Tabitha smiled to herself. Aunt Allie had lived in Colorado for most her adult life, but her southern roots ran deep.

The little shop had closed at seven today, but starting in two days, the day after Thanksgiving, they would be staying open until nine. The traffic would pick up then, both foot and car, and they would need all their stock on the shelves.

"I don't mind," Tabitha assured her. "I like keeping busy."

Aunt Allie studied her over the glasses perched on the tip of her nose. Tabitha willed herself not to squirm. The older woman looked like a grandmother, but her mind was sharp as a tack, and she was one of the kindest and most generous people Tabitha had ever met. "I suppose you do," Aunt Allie said. "Well, if it's all the same to you, I'm going to go on up and get ready for bed. I can finish decorating this tree tomorrow."

Going on impulse, Tabitha went over and put her arms around her mother's sister.

"What's this now?" Aunt Allie asked, hugging her back, "Don't you worry. You're in a safe place now."

"I'm sorry," Tabitha said, a little caught off guard by the tears that welled behind her eyelids. At thirty-two, it had been a long time since she'd had to ask anyone for help, but it had taken only one phone call to secure a safe haven here in the little mountain town of Estes Park.

"Meow," interjected Lucy, Aunt Allie's snowshoe cat, wrapping herself around their ankles as though she, too, wanted to be part of the hug. Lucy roamed the shop when she wasn't upstairs sleeping in one of the beds. There were a couple of customers who swore they came in just to visit with Lucy.

Laughing, they pulled away, the serious moment broken.

"I'm going stay up a while longer," Tabitha said as Aunt Allie double-checked to make sure the front door was locked and the blinds tightly closed.

Aunt Allie's book and coffee shop, The Book Nook, smelled of an intoxicating mixture of book dust and coffee. Customers were welcome to have a cup of coffee or hot chocolate, curl up in the large comfy chairs, and read a book from the shelves. Of course, they usually ended up buying whatever it was they were reading, which was the whole point.

There were also plenty of gifts and souvenirs scattered around for them to purchase, mugs and whatnot, especially now at the holiday season. After tomorrow, there would be a whole lot more "whatnot" to choose from.

Aunt Allie had seemed relieved to have Tabitha there to help out when she'd shown up on her doorstep last Sunday, and she had even insisted on paying Tabitha for her help. Tabitha had just been grateful to have a place to escape to. They had yet to agree on whether or not Tabitha would be paid.

Tabitha went back to the storeroom to do a little straightening up before leaving her project for the night. She was just about to head up the stairs to the apartment area of the building, when she heard a man's voice outside the back door. She froze, listening. Though she could hear his voice, she couldn't make out the words. The voice was unfamiliar. Inching to the back door, she peeked outside as she checked the lock. There was a man standing with his back to her, his cell phone pressed against his ear.

She breathed an audible sigh of relief. She was jumpy. No denying that.

The man laughed, and she smiled a little. He sounded friendly enough.

Clicking off his phone, he went inside the neighbor's back door. There had been a time, not so long ago, when she might have looked forward to meeting her aunt's neighbors, but not at this point in her life.

She double-checked the door lock before going upstairs. The shop, located on Main Street, Estes Park, Colorado, was unique and historic, a least a hundred years old. The floors, along with the walls, were made up of sturdy old timbers that had weathered the ravages of time, including at least two floods. The building, one of many in a row, was three to four times deeper than it was wide – sort of like a really long hallway. The store part was up front near the street, and the back opened into a shared courtyard. Also, at the back of the store, was a stairwell leading upstairs to a full apartment area.

Downtown consisted of rows of such shops all connected together, with occasional breaks for side streets. Over the years, some walls had been knocked out to give some owners more space. Others, like Aunt Allie's, maintained their original size, despite the closeness of neighbors. Tabitha supposed that when the town was first designed, this gave each owner a little bit of street exposure while being large enough to hold inventory.

Aunt Allie's upstairs apartment had three bedrooms, two

baths, a full kitchen, and a living area. It was small, but laid out in such a way that it didn't feel crowded. In fact, a few years ago, Aunt Allie had knocked out a wall allowing the kitchen to flow into the living area. She'd also added a curved nook off the kitchen for a breakfast area. The nook had taken up half of her back deck, but the deck was rarely used. The window nook was almost completely glass, allowing an uninterrupted view of the snow-topped mountains in the distance.

Tabitha went to her bedroom, got into her flannel pajamas, and climbed under her down comforter. It was cold, and according to the Weather Channel, it was going to get colder - unseasonably so - over the next couple of days.

The next morning, she woke to the smell of fresh coffee brewing. As had quickly become her routine, she jumped into the shower and blow-dried her long hair, that her color stylist in Boulder called "mocha latte with caramel highlights." Tabitha smiled whenever she thought about it. She found it funny having a hair color named after her favorite coffee. She smeared on some light foundation. Since it was Thanksgiving and she was feeling a bit festive, she put some sparkly brown eye shadow on her lids and added some black eyeliner and mascara to highlight her green eyes. To complete the effect, she smeared some clear lip gloss over her pink lips. Make-up wasn't popular out here in the west, but like her aunt, Tabitha had southern roots that ran deep.

Dressed and ready for the day, she made her way down the hall to where Aunt Allie would be scrambling eggs and frying bacon. She would have fresh-made biscuits coming out of the oven.

Tabitha considered the breakfasts alone payment enough for anything she did to help out around the store.

Halfway down the hallway, she stopped and listened. It was that laugh.

It was him.

Her mind circled around. How could the man she'd heard talking on his cell phone before she went up to bed last night be standing in her aunt's kitchen first thing this morning?

She stopped in the doorway to watch the interaction. The man not only had a nice laugh, but he was pleasant to look at. He looked to be about mid-thirties. A good age for men, she mused.

Then he turned and looked at her, his eyes smiling into hers. He was clean-shaven, but appeared to have skipped shaving today. He had that boy-next-door-with-an-edge look. He had a nice smile, but it was his eyes that had her heart skipping a beat.

"Hi," he said.

"Hi," she echoed.

"Oh, good," Aunt Allie said, turning away from the stove. "Tabitha, this is Adam Patton, from next door. Adam, this is my niece, Tabitha."

"Happy Thanksgiving," he said.

Thanksgiving. Right. "It's nice to meet you."

"Adam brought over some fresh-squeezed orange juice."

Obviously knowing his way around Aunt Allie's kitchen, Adam took a glass from the cabinet, filled it with orange juice, and handed it to her. His fingers brushed hers as she took it from him, and she flinched, but then grasped the glass to keep from dropping it. Had he noticed?

"Sorry about that," he said. Obviously, he had noticed.

"It's okay. It was my fault."

"Adam, pull up a chair and have breakfast with us," Aunt Allie said, putting the finishing touches on an omelet.

"Thanks, Aunt Allie," he said, "but my mother will kill me if I'm late for Thanksgiving brunch." He glanced at his watch. "I should get going. I'll stop in later. Nice to meet you, Tabitha," he said with a wide grin, as he left, leaving behind a whiff of male cologne that had Tabitha watching after him.

Pulling her attention back, Tabitha sat down at the kitchen table. "Where did he come from?" she asked. Her heart was beating a little fast, but not in a "panic attack" kind of fast.

"I'm sorry. I didn't mention him, did I?" she asked, putting a plate heaped with an omelet, bacon, and toast in front of Tabitha. "He has a shop next door; mostly things for guys like fishing tackle and such. In fact, he ties his own fishing flies. He sells to people all over the country. Has an Internet site, which we should look into. Anyway, he comes over quite a bit to help out with things and such. He replaced one of those old electric plugs downstairs, so he helps out and keeps me company."

"What about your ladies' group?"

"Oh, they're fine for lunches and things. Sometimes it's just nice to have a man around," She beamed at Tabitha. "And a good-looking one, too."

Tabitha took a bite of bacon as she considered this. She usually grabbed a breakfast bar on her way out the door as she headed to work. Between the breakfast and Adam's cologne, she was in sensory overload. Her aunt was right, though. Adam was, indeed, good-looking. "How does his wife feel about him spending all that time over here with an older woman?" she asked, teasing her aunt a little.

Aunt Allie giggled, as she sat next to Tabitha. "He's not married, and never has been."

"Is he gay?"

"Oh, Heavens, no," she took a bite of eggs, considered. "At least I don't think so. No," she decided. "He used to date that little Cosby girl from over at Longmont. I'm not sure what happened, but it was a bad breakup. I don't think he's dated seriously ever since."

"Hmm," Tabitha said, as her aunt moved on to the next topic, leaving many unanswered questions about this mysterious neighbor. Aunt Allie wanted to put some things into storage to have more room for Tabitha. Her aunt had been using the two guest rooms as overflow closets, but with Tabitha's help, she had cleared out one of the bedrooms, at least enough for Tabitha to have plenty of space. Tabitha had already assured her at least three times that she wasn't worried about the clutter.

Besides, in less than six weeks, she would be going home to her condo. She mentally ticked off her calendar. She would drive back to Boulder after New Year's, then return to work January eighth, five days after her court date. January third was a date seared into her brain. In six weeks, she would be divorced.

With it being Thanksgiving, they didn't open the shop that day, but instead, spent it getting things ready for Black Friday. They put up sale signs here and there to entice people to go after the good deals.

"If you really want to start a web site," Tabitha told her at onc point as they took a break and went upstairs to the kitchen to make an apple-and-cranberry pie. "I can do that for you."

"Really? You know how to do that?"

"I'm pretty sure I can figure it out."

Aunt Allie clasped her hands together in front of her. "Oh, that would be so wonderful. I'll pay you extra for that."

"Aunt Allie, I wish you wouldn't pay me for anything. I'm just grateful to have a place to stay for awhile."

"Are you kidding? You are truly a gem. I just have to figure out how to keep you here."

Tabitha smiled. As much as she liked it here at her aunt's, her life was back at the University of Colorado.

"Are you sure your department chair won't let you stay a few more months? Maybe through the spring semester?

"Ha." Tabitha switched from peeling green apples to slicing them into little chunks. "He went above and beyond by letting me finish out this semester teaching online. He made me promise to be back for spring semester.

"You never said," Aunt Allie begin pressing dough into a pie shell. "Does he know about your... situation?"

Tabitha swept a wisp of hair from her cheek with her wrist. "He knows about Bobby, alright. It was after Bobby showed up in my classroom that he actually asked if there was anywhere I could go for awhile."

Tabitha rinsed the apples and laid them on paper towels to dry as the familiar range of emotions swept through her. Anger. Sadness. Disappointment. She had made a good career for herself teaching American history at the University of Colorado.

"Well, I'm thankful you thought of me."

Tabitha took a deep breath and glanced at Aunt Allie with a smile. "It gave me a good excuse to visit you. It's been too long. Besides, you live at the gateway to the Rocky Mountains."

"We do have the best views," Aunt Allie agreed.

Tabitha heard the pride in her aunt's voice. "That is something pretty amazing." Tabitha put the apples in a bowl, added a teaspoon of cinnamon, two tablespoons of flour, a dash of nutmeg, and a sprinkle of sugar. Aunt Allie handed her the crust, lined with half a dozen thin pats of butter. Tabitha poured the apple mixture into the crust, then added a heaping cup of cranberries.

Aunt Allie put some more pats of butter on the top, then crisscrossed strips of crust across the top of the pie.

After putting the pie in the oven, they were cleaning up the kitchen, when someone knocked at the back door. Tabitha dropped the plate she was holding and little pieces of glass scattered over the floor. Her heart racing, she apologized profusely, on the verge of tears.

"It'll just be Adam," Aunt Allie told her, her voice calm. "I'll go outside and stall him a few minutes while you get yourself together."

"I'm ok. I'll clean this mess up," she said again. "I am so sorry I broke a plate."

"It's okay," Aunt Allie assured her. "It can happen to anyone."

Tabitha locked Lucy in one of the bedrooms so she wouldn't get glass in her paws and cleaned up the glass. She was just putting away the broom when she heard Adam and Aunt Allie coming inside.

"Where's Lucy?" Adam asked. "I brought her a present."

"I'll get her," Tabitha said, rushing to the bedroom. She barely had the door cracked, when the cat raced past her toward the kitchen. Apparently, Adam had brought her presents before.

"I brought you something, too," Adam said to Tabitha.

"Me? Why?" Tabitha said, her heart rate tripping up a notch.

He shrugged. "Why not? It's one of my mom's home-made pumpkin pies."

"Oh, those are just wonderful," Aunt Allie said.

"We have an apple-cranberry pie in the oven," Tabitha told him.

"Then save mine for later," he said, handing her the pie.

"Only if you come back later and have some with us," she said, then quickly bit her lip, surprising herself with the spontaneous invitation.

He smiled at Tabitha, and her heart gave a little stutter. It was a sensation she had nearly forgotten existed.

"I'll do it," he said. "But only if I can have a piece of that apple pie."

"It's a deal," Aunt Allie agreed. "But since it's going to be about an hour before it's ready, why don't we go downstairs, and you can help out with a little project Tabitha and I have going?"

Tabitha shot a glance toward Adam and shrugged her shoulders. Aunt Allie was the guru of projects, which was probably the reason her shop was so successful. She thought of things to do. And she got things done.

"Sure," Adam said. "Whatever you need."

They followed Aunt Allie downstairs. There was still a lot of preparation to go. Tabitha squared her shoulders and took a deep breath. There were boxes scattered everywhere, half-open with garland and faux snow spilling out everywhere. There were glass ornaments and scented pinecones, stockings, and wrapping paper.

"It's kind of a mess," Aunt Allie commented.

"It's a process," Tabitha said. "But we do have a lot to do before morning."

"What can I do?" Adam asked.

Aunt Allie and Tabitha both turned toward the tree, a twelve-foot balsam fir draped with clear lights.

Tabitha went to one of the boxes and carefully pulled out a two-foot-tall angel with glittering silver wings, a shimmering gown with lace and silk, a fur-trimmed stole, and trails of silver ribbons.

"She came west with the wagons," Aunt Allie said.

"I recognize her," Adam said, studying the top of the tree. He rubbed his chin. "We're gonna need a ladder," he said.

"There's one out in the shed," Aunt Allie said, and Adam promptly went out back to get the ladder.

"She's beautiful," Tabitha said, fluffing the angel's lace and ribbons. "It's a shame she has to live in a box for all but six weeks of the year."

"I suppose we could find a place for her up on one of the top shelves," Aunt Allie mused. "But I think she's safer in the box. I just want to protect her, you know?"

"I understand. She's irreplaceable. And it's special when you take her out each Thanksgiving."

Aunt Allie beamed as Adam came back inside with an eight-foot step ladder. "Looks like this ladder has seen better days," he said, opening up the ladder.

"Well, I don't usually have any use for it."

"Who put this angel up there last year?"

"You did," Aunt Allie said.

"Guess I've slept since then," Adam said, holding out his hands for the angel.

Tabitha hesitated, cradling the fragile ornament in her hand.

"You know what?" she said. "I think I'd like to put her up there."

Adam shifted his gaze from the ladder to the top of the tree. "I don't think it's a good idea for you to be climbing up there on this ladder."

"I know, but... "she shrugged. "This angel is older than all of us put together."

Shaking his head, he moved to the side of the ladder. "You won't mind if I hold the ladder for you?"

She smiled and looked up at him. "I was kind of counting on it."

"Here," Aunt Allie said, stepping forward. "Let me hold the angel."

Tabitha handed the ornament over to Aunt Allie and stepped onto the first rung of the ladder. It felt a little unsteady. "We don't have another ladder?" She was high enough now to look directly into Adam's eyes – deep pools of slate blue. Mesmerized, she wobbled the ladder. He immediately placed a hand on the small of her back to steady her.

Aunt Allie shook her head.

"You don't have a better ladder?" She vaguely heard Aunt Allie ask Adam.

He pulled his gaze away to glance at his watch. "If the hardware store was open, I could be back in thirty minutes with one. But it's closed today."

"That's okay. I can do this," Tabitha said, shifting her focus to the task at hand.

"I'll have one next time," he said.

Tabitha moved to the next step. The ladder wobbled, but Adam kept it steady. She took a deep breath and put a foot on next step. Her fingers dug into the coarse wood of the old ladder. The top of the tree was still too far away. "I have to keep going," she said, mostly to herself.

She went up two more rungs. She took a deep, steadying breath and looked down at Adam. His legs were apart, both hands firmly on the ladder.

"You sure you don't want me to do this?" he asked.

"I've got it," she said and went up the next two levels. *Don't think about it. Don't look down.*

One step away from the top of the ladder now, she was high enough to reach the top of the tree. Unfortunately, it was going to be a stretch to reach the center of the top of the tree. She hadn't taken that into account.

She looked down at Aunt Allie. Lowered her arm for the angel. Aunt Allie stretched, but she was too far.

"I'll bring it up," Aunt Allie said.

Adam groaned.

Aunt Allie went up two rungs until she was high enough to hand Tabitha the delicate ornament.

Now Tabitha had one hand clutching the ladder and the ornament in the other. This had been a really bad idea.

She sighed. She was in it now. Her right hand digging into the wood of the ladder, she used her left hand to place the angel over the top of the tree.

"You did it!" Aunt Allie said. "Come down now."

"Wait," Tabitha said, "I have to straighten it up." With one hand, she fluffed out the skirt of the angel and arranged the flowing white ribbons.

"Got it now?" Adam asked, his voice strained.

"How does it look?"

"It looks perfect," Aunt Allie said.

Tabitha began to back down the ladder. The wood creaked. "See," she said. "You were worried for nothing."

On the third rung from the ground, the wooden step splintered, and Tabitha lost her footing. She gasped as the step broke, and she slipped.

Before she knew what was happening, she was in Adam's arms. He kept them both upright and slid her to her feet. The softness of his sweatshirt pressed against her cheek, the abs beneath were surprisingly taut.

Her heart slammed against her chest as she leaned against him, her fingers digging into his arms.

Aunt Allie put a hand on Tabitha's arm. "Are you alright?"

"I think so," she said against Adam's shoulder. "Nice catch," she said, assured that both feet were safely on the ground. Despite the assurance of safety, her heart raced.

"I didn't do two tours in Afghanistan for nothing," he said.

"You were military?" She breathed. *Focus.*

"Air Force," he said. "Come on, let's bandage up your hands."

Tabitha looked at her hands. She hadn't realized she'd gotten scratched up and was bleeding now.

"There's a first aid kit in the break room," Aunt Allie said.

Tabitha followed Adam to the break room at the back of the store. He took the little first-aid box from the cabinet.

She didn't even ask how he knew where to find it. "Let's wash your hands," he said, urging her to the sink.

"Were you an officer?" she asked.

"Para-rescue," he said, taking her right hand and examining it. "No splinters in this one. Let me see the other one."

"Seriously? How many years?" Except for the surprising firmness of the muscles under his sweatshirt, he didn't look military.

"Six. No splinters. It's not as bad as it looks."

She swallowed thickly at the feel of his hands on hers. He gently patted her hands dry with a clean paper towel, then applied antibiotic ointment to the scratches.

She lifted her gaze to his and stared into his deep blue eyes. And found herself smiling back at him.

Seconds passed before she realized he held both her hands in his. His thumb grazed her finger, and she jumped back, sliding her hands away from his.

"I should, um," she tore her gaze from his and swallowed thickly. "I should check on the pie." She turned blindly and dashed up the kitchen stairs.

Aunt Allie was already in the kitchen pulling the pie from the oven. Tabitha thought she had been with Adam only moments.

"There you are," she said, taking the hot pad mitts from her hands. Perhaps it hadn't been so very long. "How's your hand?"

Tabitha had forgotten all about the scratches. She glanced down, felt a flush on her cheeks. "Good," she said.

Aunt Allie looked at her with an odd expression. "Where's Adam? The pie is ready."

"I think he went home," she said.

"Are you kidding?" He said behind her. "And miss this pie? Not a chance."

Tabitha bit her lip and kept herself busy gathering plates and forks, then helping Aunt Allie put the pie on the plates.

They sat at the little breakfast table in the glass nook with a view of the courtyard. Aunt Allie and Adam swapped stories about Black Fridays from the past.

"I hope this one goes off without any hitches," Aunt Allie said.

"I'm sure it will," Adam said optimistically.

"We still have a lot to do," Tabitha commented, thinking about the inventory left to put on the shelves.

"As long as we put it somewhere," Aunt Allie said, "We can rearrange it tomorrow. In fact, I'm sure we'll be rearranging a lot over the next few weeks."

When they finished their pie, Tabitha gathered up the plates, rinsed them, and put them in the dishwasher, while Adam brought a box of cat litter upstairs for Aunt Allie. The cat litter turned into moving cartons of bottled water and a few other things upstairs.

Tabitha disappeared downstairs to begin putting inventory on the shelves. She did not want to be up all night.

Chapter 2

Switching on the evening news, Adam was reminded that, yes, tomorrow would be an early day for him as a shop owner, though truth be told, his shop catered toward the masculine shopper, and they tended to not get up before the chickens the day after Thanksgiving to seek out a bargain. But alas, some would be dragged along by their women and would seek a haven in his shop. Nonetheless, like the other shops, tomorrow should be a good day.

Rover, his trusty golden retriever, climbed into his lap and watched him watch the news. Adam idly scratched his ears.

Though he knew he'd be getting to bed early tonight, he wasn't the least bit sleepy. Not with images of Aunt Allie's niece dancing in his head. To think she'd been there nearly a week, and he hadn't caught sight of her. He had some making up to do.

She was truly a vision of sugar plums.

He shook his head at the direction of his thoughts. The Christmas season hadn't even really started yet, and he had yet to get into the eggnog.

That was the plight of the shop owner, he supposed. Preparing for the season before anyone else had given it much thought at all.

Thank goodness he had two college students to take care of the decorating details downstairs in the store. If he had to do it all by himself, he would, indeed, go crazy. However... if he had Tabitha to help...

Not that he was interested in getting involved with anyone. Besides, he'd best tread carefully. It wouldn't do to get involved with Aunt Allie's niece, of all people. If it didn't go well, it could strain his relationship with Aunt Allie.

Vulnerable. That was how he would describe Tabitha Black in one word. Vulnerable and fragile if given two. Something had happened to her. He didn't know what, of course, but whatever it was set off his protective instincts.

With a sigh, he switched off the television and went down the hall to his bedroom. His place was a mirror image of Aunt Allie's, except for the improvements that had been done over the years. At some point, probably several decades ago, the two apartments had been part of the same house. Then, through the years, it had been divided and transformed into what it was today. Two shops with two living apartments on the second floor. Not a bad deal, really. He didn't have to commute. He could run down to the shop in the middle of the night in his pajamas if he wanted to. Or he could leave the shop and run upstairs to take a nap, which had been known to happen on too many occasions to speak of. Or maybe to watch a hockey game. Or maybe a hockey game and a nap at the same time.

He actually enjoyed tying his fishing lures and selling them over the Internet more than anything else. He'd sort of gotten saddled with the shop in what he considered an unfair way.

But such was the way of life; his anyway. Nobody ever said life was fair.

His father had given Adam the space to create his own business, as long as he also kept up the family shop, "The Fishing Cove." Adam liked fishing lures. He merely tolerated the duck decoys and deer stands. He especially didn't care for the line of hunting outfits. No special clothing required for tossing a lure into the lake, except maybe some waders. Unfortunately, he didn't sell enough to stock them.

Right now all he wanted was to fall asleep. Though he fell asleep easily enough, it was almost three in the morning when he woke in a cold sweat.

Her Christmas Rescue

Chapter 3
Emma

Tabitha woke at 3:00 a.m. in a cold sweat. By now, she knew the drill. It was a rare night when she didn't have a nightmare in one form or another. Tonight's was different, but typical. She'd been in an elevator, alone, when it started to crash. She'd fallen, crashing to the earth, only to get up and have someone after her. She had run away, hiding behind curtains, boxes, anything, always knowing that he was behind her. That he would find her.

Then, as always, she had awakened, trembling and exhausted. It was no way to sleep.

She was so tired of the dreams. She wanted to just go to sleep and *sleep*, without the demons.

She jumped when Lucy landed on the bed next to her. The cat

meowed and snuggled her face next to Tabitha's. With the gentle purring from the cat, Tabitha began to relax, and her racing heart rate returned to normal.

She was safe here, she reminded herself. Bobby couldn't get to her here. He'd never cared enough to learn much about her family, so he wouldn't know where to look for her.

He probably wouldn't care to look for her anyway, she thought, cynically. He'd made it pretty clear what he thought about her.

She sighed. It was better this way. Truly it was. But how did someone go from making life plans to stay together forever to - she stopped herself, shaking her head.

And got out of bed.

She padded down the hall to the kitchen, Lucy following at her feet, and turned on the coffee pot. Flipping on the little TV that sat on the counter, she made herself some coffee, stirring in creamer until it no longer tasted like coffee.

"Sorry, Lucy, no midnight snack for you," she said, tucking her feet under the kitchen chair and switching to the Weather Channel.

The local forecast was actually predicting below-freezing temperatures for this weekend, during the day. It was already below freezing at night, but in the forties during the day. Having grown up in Houston, Tabitha had rarely seen snow until she'd moved up here. In fact, just the mention of snow or ice would automatically shut down the city of Houston. She'd been teaching at University of Colorado for four years, but the sight of snow was still magical.

Maybe she should go down and light a fire in the fireplace in the morning. The coziness of the burning wood should bring in a few customers and cause some to linger and perhaps make a purchase. It was a good idea.

She glanced at the kitchen clock. If they were really going to open at six a.m. as advertised, they only had three hours to get ready.

She molded her hand to the coffee mug and considered. If she went ahead and brought in the wood now, she could take a shower and get herself ready to face the day, and still have time to open up the store, all with a fire blazing in the fireplace.

Wearing her dark blue plaid flannel pajamas and gray UGGS booties, she turned on the light to the patio and peeked outside. The firewood was only a few feet away to the left. Lucy threaded herself around her legs and meowed.

Unlocking the door, she eased it open, nudging Lucy back with her foot. She couldn't leave the door open, or Lucy would get out. She stepped outside, shivered, and almost changed her mind. But the thought of a cozy fire motivated her to keep going. Maybe she should go back and grab a coat.

She let the door bump against the frame, not quite closing all the way. She dashed over, loaded her arms with firewood, and headed back. The cold air ignored her flannel pajamas going straight to her bones. Reaching the door, she turned to nudge the door open with her shoulder. Nudged. Then shoved.

Then panicked. When had the door closed? She hadn't heard it. Her hands were too full to try the doorknob. She shifted the wood to have one hand free. Turned the doorknob.

Then dropped the wood with a loud clamor. Twisted the doorknob again now with both hands. It didn't move.

Aunt Allie had one of *those* door locks. Oh Crap! It was about twenty-eight degrees outside according to the Weather Channel. She would freeze to death out here.

Her mind raced. She didn't have her keys and couldn't get inside. Couldn't get into her car. Didn't even have her cell phone.

She stood there for a moment, feeling the cold from the concrete seep past her little house slippers. The wind cut through her flannel pajamas.

This could be considered an emergency.

She pounded on the door. Waited. Heard Lucy meowing. Any other time, this might have actually been amusing; her locked out and Lucy meowing on the other side of the door.

She pounded again.

Waited. Aunt Allie's bedroom was at the front of the house. There was no way she would hear her.

And there was no way Tabitha was going to go around to Main Street in her pajamas to knock on the front door. Not even at four in the morning.

She knocked again, louder this time.

Again.

She was cold. She wondered how long she could survive.

She looked around, and a different kind of fear shot through her.

This one wasn't about the cold. This was about being outside in the middle of the night. Vulnerable.

A dog howled somewhere. A car door slammed. She shivered.

And pounded on the door.

Keep Reading
***Her Christmas Rescue*...**

Kathryn Kaleigh writes sweet contemporary romance, time travel romance, and historical romance.

kathrynkaleigh.com

www.ingramcontent.com/pod-product-compliance
Lightning Source LLC
Chambersburg PA
CBHW061512120726
48001CB00004B/1303